W9-BZH-061

WINTER OF THE WOLF
by G. Clifton Wisler

A story is told, in the lands along the upper Brazos River, a story that speaks of great courage, of great sacrifice. It concerns two boys not yet full grown and the legend of a Comanche devil spirit. It is said to have taken place during the winter of 1864, when the times were full of violence, and great demands were made of boys as well as of men. For that winter is remembered, by those who have heard the story, as the winter of the wolf.

T.J. was only fourteen that year, when his father and two older brothers rode off to fight the Yankees under General Hood, but he was the man of the family then, so it was up to him to guard the womanfolk and keep the homestead going.

The Comanches begin to raid the unprotected settlements, but more deadly by far to T.J. and his family is a huge and sinister wolf, which seems immune to bullets. One night T.J. fires at the marauding animal point-blank, and it escapes unhurt. A young Comanche he has befriended tells him that it is not a living wolf at all but a demon—an evil spirit of Comanche legend. Together the two boys set out to kill the mysterious monster.

Readers will be enthralled by this dramatic story of the Texas frontier and an eerie legend that haunted it.

G. Clifton Wisler

WINTER OF THE WOLF

ELSEVIER/NELSON BOOKS
New York

DIXON PUBLIC LIBRARY
DIXON ILLINOIS

131662

No character in this book is intended to
represent any actual person; all the incidents of the
story are entirely fictional in nature.

Copyright © 1981 by G. Clifton Wisler
All rights reserved. No part of this publication may
be reproduced or transmitted in any form or by any means,
electronic or mechanical, including photocopy, recording,
or any information storage and retrieval system
now known or to be invented, without permission in writing
from the publisher, except by a reviewer who wishes
to quote brief passages in connection with a review written
for inclusion in a magazine, newspaper, or broadcast.

Library of Congress Cataloging in Publication Data

Wisler, G Clifton.
Winter of the wolf.
SUMMARY: In charge of the family's Texas homestead
during the Civil War, 14-year-old T.J. saves the life of
a Comanche boy during an Indian raid and they subse-
quently hunt a large, silver wolf purported to be the
devil.
[1. Frontier and pioneer life—Fiction. 2. Comanche
Indians—Fiction. 3. Indians of North America—Fiction.
4. Wolves—Fiction] I. Title.
PZ7.W78033Wi   1981   [Fic]   80–21851
ISBN 0–525–66716–4

Published in the United States by Elsevier/Nelson Books,
a division of Elsevier-Dutton Publishing Company, Inc.,
New York. Published simultaneoulsy in Don Mills,
Ontario, by Nelson/Canada.

Printed in the U.S.A.   First Edition
10 9 8 7 6 5 4 3 2 1

J

(ll -)

BSB 4-23-81 $7.94

This book is dedicated to
Mrs. Judy Jeffress,
teacher and friend,
whose encouragement and enthusiasm
have been a source of strength.

About This Book

The lands that are watered by the upper Brazos River are hard lands. The soil is rocky, and in the summer even the rattlesnakes shrink from the fiery sun. In the times before white men came there, Indian tribes used to live along the cliffs of the canyons. There are some who believe their spirits dwell there still.

In the years after Texas became part of the United States, white men from Tennessee and Alabama, Virginia and the Carolinas, Pennsylvania and Indiana came to the waters of the Brazos to farm and raise cattle.

They found life there difficult, but they stayed,

scratching out their lives even as the scrub mesquite and yucca had done for centuries before.

The land demands much of those who claim it. It is a land of tall men, of tall deeds. Weak men are swallowed up by the heat and the rock and the loneliness. A hundred stories written in blood and etched in sweat or echoed beneath a winter's moonlight tell of the courage of the men and the harshness of the land. There are some who say these stories hold no truth. There are those who say they do.

Of all the stories that are told, there is one which speaks of the greatest courage, the greatest sacrifice. It is about two boys not yet full grown and the legend of a Comanche devil spirit. It is said to have taken place during the winter of 1864, when the times were full of violence, and great demands were made of boys as well as of men. That winter is remembered by some who have heard the story as the winter of the wolf.

1

I was only fourteen years old in August of 1864. It was a time I was to remember well, for it signaled the end of those years I lived as a boy and the beginning of the years I was to live as a man.

The summer of '64 was especially hot, even for Texas. The sun burned and scorched the earth until I thought one day I might shrivel up under its blaze the way our corn did.

Ours was a small homestead on the upper Brazos, and we worked the rocky soil hard for the few bushels of corn that kept us alive. In the open pasture along the river, we grazed the small herd of cattle that would pay for our clothing and the few tools that needed replacing each year.

In the fall, after harvesting the corn, my father, brothers, and I would hunt in the deer thicket for a buck or two and some rabbits and other small game. And there were always fish to be caught in the river.

Between our small farmhouse and the barn, my mother had planted a generous assortment of all those greens which I never could really tolerate— spinach and cabbage and such. Just to keep harmony in the family, she had added some carrots and sugar beets, and even some melons.

We were a close family, for our neighbors were few and far between. They kept mainly to themselves, but then I suppose we did, too. We were a large family, as was usual in Texas, for there were always chores to be done. Besides my mother and father, there were my two grown brothers, Jackson and Houston; my sisters Abigail, Rachel, and Hope; and my little brothers Travis and Austin. And me, of course.

As you can tell, all the boys were named for famous men. That's how I got my name, Thomas Jefferson Clinton. That's a very big name for a boy, so I cut it down a bit to T.J. Ma alone called me Thomas, and Pa called me Thomas Jefferson when I'd messed up something.

For a while, my sister Sarah and her husband Stewart lived with us, but they'd packed up and headed for the Oregon Territory back in 1860. We also used to have Grandpa and Grandma Clinton, but the hard winter of '62 took them with it, as Pa always said.

We still had Grandma Nelson with us, though. She must have been near eighty by my estimate, and I stayed clear of her. She was always yelling at me to take a bath or keep clear of her rug or something. Ma liked having her around, though, so I made allowances.

August was not a good month for any of us. I spent most of my time carrying buckets of water from the river to the cornfields, trying to keep the plants alive. I could run my hand along the nearly ripe husks and feel how hard and dry the corn was. I hoped we'd get enough of a crop to keep us from starving.

We had more than the weather to worry about, though. In the middle of August, a messenger rode up to our house. He was dressed in a colorful uniform—light gray with buttercup cuffs and shiny braid running up his sleeves. He had a letter from the government in Austin calling to arms all men over the age of eighteen.

Pa read the letter, offered the messenger a ladle of water, and began polishing the barrel of his rifle. That night he called us all together.

"There's a call to arms," Pa told us. "It calls every able-bodied man to take his rifle and make his way to Houston City. From there we will go on to Tennessee to help General Hood fight Yankees."

"You have to go?" asked Ma.

I saw in her eyes what she was thinking. Ever since the Yankees started marching into Virginia four years before, men from the little farms along the Brazos had ridden off to join the army. None of them had returned.

"My pa fought with Sam Houston at San Jacinto," Pa said, looking into our eyes. "I served in the war against Mexico and was with Winfield Scott when he took Veracruz. Was shot twice, but still marched into Mexico City with the rest of the men. I don't rightly like to leave you all, but I see it as a duty, and I've fought too hard all my life to turn away from a bunch of Yankees."

"You have to?" asked Abigail.

"It's a man's duty to fight for his land, defend his home. He has to march beside the flag of his people and his nation."

"Then you must take your warmest clothing," said Ma, not a tear in her eye. "I've heard there's a chill in the mountains of Tennessee, and the winters are powerful cold."

"If you must go, Pa," said Jackson, "then Houston and I are bound to ride with you. We've got less of a right to stay than you, for we have no wives or children."

"It's the truth," said Ma, shaking a little. "If I could, I'd keep you from the face of war. My brother died at Veracruz, shot not five feet from where your Pa stood. I'd have spared you that. But you are men, as you say, and I've no right to hold you back from the world."

"And me, Pa?" I asked. "I'm fourteen. I'm old enough to go, too."

"I'll not leave my women completely without defense," Pa said, putting his great weathered hand on my shoulder. "You are still not half grown, and your ma will need you to help with the fields. I say this to you, son. You face a tougher enemy in this land than we face in a hundred muskets."

I smiled as he said that, pleased he knew I would take care of things. But there was a fear in me, too, for I suddenly found myself responsible for the lives of seven people.

We ate a hearty dinner that evening, but I noticed Ma ate very little. I heard her crying later that night, and I wondered how she always kept those things she felt bottled up inside her.

Pa and Houston and Jackson helped me get in the corn crop before they rode off to Houston City to join the Confederate army. They took all but one of our horses, an old nag named Cactus. I followed their dust with my eyes until it passed from view. Then I turned away, concentrating on the things that were to be done.

Ma and the girls tended the garden, but there was only my younger brother Travis, ten years old, to help me mind the cattle and do all the other chores. There was so much to be done, and it seemed my hands were too small to get it done. But there is something within a man that grows fiercest when the odds are greatest. That something was within my father at Veracruz, my grandfather at San Jacinto, and I knew it was within me, too.

2

September found us happy and secure in our little farmhouse on the banks of the Brazos. The crib was full of corn, quickly harvested by my father and brothers before they left, and there had been enough besides to trade with neighbors for some fresh fruit and extra shot and powder.

I found myself more and more alone as the days went on. My brother Travis had taken to fishing, leaving me to tend the cattle alone. The girls were completing their gardening and feeding the chickens and pigs. Ma and Grandma Nelson kept busy sewing and spinning. There was a lot of cotton available since the port at New Orleans had been closed, and some small mills had sprung up in Texas. But there were many women like Ma who chose to spin the raw cotton into thread and make their own fabrics.

I hoped to increase our clothing supply that fall by shooting some deer. Travis, Austin, and I could wear buckskin. All three of us were excited by the thought, and I already had plans for new deerskin gloves, jacket, and trousers. We would soon slaughter some cattle, and I'd talked to Mr. Einsbruch, one of our neighbors, about curing the hides. A new pair of leather boots was badly needed, as my old ones were nearly worn through.

There was a new danger in the air, though. The Comanche Indians, aware our men were fighting to the east, decided to raid the settlements south of the Red River. All sorts of terrifying stories were coming in about scalpings and kidnappings. I heard a particularly frightening story of the torture of a boy my age from Nels Einsbruch.

There was much talk of raising a company of militia to fight the Comanches, should they appear in our area. Mr. Einsbruch was in favor of the idea, and most of the remaining men in the valley had signed up. No one had asked me yet, but I knew Ma had heard about it, since she was acting nervous again.

One day I found her chasing a chicken out of her garden. She was giving that chicken a lecture like I'd never heard. She finally told it that if it got back into her garden, it would be chicken and dumplings for dinner come Sunday.

I doubled over with laughter, coughing in delight.

"Just what are you laughing at, Thomas?" she asked me. "Perhaps I should be chasing you instead of this poor dumb chicken."

"You look so funny," I laughed. "You remind me of Grandma Nelson when I step on her rug."

"You mind you behave yourself around your grandma," she lectured me.

"I do, Ma," I said, swallowing the last bit of laughter.

"Oh, I've spoiled your fun, Thomas," she said, frowning. "I don't really mean to be so solemn. It's just the times and all. I believe that's the first time I've seen you laugh since your pa went to fight the war. I didn't mean to stop you."

"You haven't had much of a chance to laugh, either," I told her. "Life is going to be tough on all of us for a while."

"More on you than the rest of us," she said. "You should have had another year or two to grow. Soon enough you'll be fighting battles yourself."

"Very soon, Ma," I said. "They're raising a militia company to fight the Comanches. Each farm is expected to lend a man. I'm the closest thing we have to a man."

"That doesn't mean us," Ma said, turning away.

"Most of these farms haven't lent three men to the army. We've done our part. If they want us to send a man, then they can just bring back one of the three they've already taken away."

"You know that won't work," I said. "I have to join up. I can't expect someone else to fight the Indians while I stay here. I can shoot as good as anyone, and I can ride well when I have a decent horse under me. I'm strong for a boy, and I know how to take care of myself."

"That's not what worries me," she said. "If something happened to you, there'd be no one to get us through the winter."

"Travis is some help," I said.

"Travis can't even hold up a rifle. Your sisters are not used to shooting deer and turkey. No, Thomas," she said. "We need you."

"Ma, it's got to be done," I told her.

"Well, then do it, son. But you tell them it's only for defense. If it comes to riding off, you'll have to stay here. You tell them that, or I will."

"Yes, ma'am," I said.

We had our first assembly at the Einsbruch farm later that week. I think most of the men were surprised I was there. I didn't look like much of a soldier riding up on old Cactus, my hunting rifle slung across my shoulder. I dismounted and made my way to where Nels Einsbruch was standing.

Nels was about the closest thing I had to a friend. He was seventeen, but we both loved to hunt. I suppose he was six or seven inches taller than I was, but differences seem less important when you're doing something together.

The Einsbruchs had a big place upriver from us. Mr. Einsbruch and his wife had come over from Germany after the Republic of Texas won its independence from Mexico. They'd got a grant for land on the Brazos at the same time my grandfather got his. Then they'd bought out two neighbors.

The Einsbruchs had a big stone house, built the year before the war. Nels had four brothers, but only Hermann was still at home. The other three had joined the army in 1861. I heard that one of them had fallen at Shiloh, a second at Vicksburg.

Nels also had a sister named Bertha, who was to be avoided like a plague. Bertha used to ride over to our house and chase me all over the place. She was a year older than me, but I was the only boy close to her age for nearly forty miles.

When I got off my horse, she came running out with a glass of tea in her hand.

"Why, my poor brave T.J.," she screamed in front of everyone. "You're so brave to go riding off to battle."

"Would you please go away," I told her. "I'd rather face a hundred Comanches than have you after me."

I could hear the men laughing behind me.

"But I had to bring you some tea." she sighed. "Why, I just couldn't stand to think of you chasing down those Indians with such a parched throat. And on that horse," she sneered, shaking her head. "How can a soldier ride out against Indians with a horse like that?"

Mr. Einsbruch walked over and rescued me.

"Bertha, dear," he said. "T.J. is here on military business. You have to talk to him later. Now run on and help your mother."

"Yes, Pa," she said, grabbing my hand and giving it a parting squeeze.

When she'd left, Mr. Einsbruch gave me a knowing smile.

"Easy, son," he said. "Bertha comes on a little strong. But she's a good girl, strong and healthy. She will one day make a good wife for a farmer like you. You'll see."

"I hope not," I said, frowning.

"She's right about one thing," he said, leading me to where the others were waiting. "You need a good horse to fight Comanches. When we go out after Indians, you must borrow one of mine. You'll fight better with a good horse under you."

"Thank you, sir. But my ma made me promise not to leave the valley. She said I could fight, but she can't get through the winter without me."

"How sweet," said Ned Johnson. "My woman is all

alone at our place, too, but I don't hide behind her skirts."

"You're a fool, Johnson," said Nels. "He's got two brothers and a father in the army. He's only fourteen, and he's not hiding behind anyone. Your woman has no kids, and she has a brother living at your place who's older than T.J. I don't see him here."

"He's no use for fighting Indians," Ned said. "I think the boy still wets the bed."

I didn't laugh with the others. I knew Jimmy Hannard. I also knew they'd be saying the same things about me if I'd stayed home.

"There's no reason to talk like that," Mr. Einsbruch said. "T.J. is with us, and that is that. He represents his farm, and it is to be protected as all others. We have things to do at this meeting. First we must choose a captain."

"I'd like to nominate you, Mr. Einsbruch," said Henry Jorgenson. "You got some military experience, and, more important, you got the biggest and only stone house. If we need a fort, looks like your place'd be it."

"Agreed," said Mr. Einsbruch. "That doesn't mean I should be captain, though. We have others here who would lead as well."

"I nominate George Flowers," Ned Johnson said. "George served in the Mexican War."

"I'm too old," said Flowers, who was nearly sixty. "I don't set a horse none too good. If the weather turned cold, I couldn't even stay overnight. No, I'm not your man."

Several of the men argued over who should be captain. Finally it was narrowed down to a vote for Bret Sickles or Mr. Einsbruch. Mr. Einsbruch won the vote, and our first item of business was settled.

"Now then, men," Mr. Einsbruch addressed us. "You have all heard of Indian raids to the north. As individual farmers, we have no chance of stopping a raid. But bound together, we present our enemy with a substantial force. We must each of us keep an eye out for Indians. If you see Comanches, or even signs they have been around, do not fight. Get your family to safety and tell your nearest neighbor. That way we assemble and meet the enemy."

"But that means giving up our homes," said John French. "My father put in ten years of back-breaking labor to build our farm."

"Yes," said Bobby Henson, the oldest of the Henson boys. "That's fine for those of you here by the river. But those of us with the outlying farms will be hit first. That means being burned out, our crops destroyed."

"That's true," said Tom Hill. "My place is all alone, too, but I wouldn't have my wife and sons scalped just to satisfy my father's labor. Farmhouses can be rebuilt. We can only protect the women by banding together. And don't forget, there are men like John Clinton who have been here since the beginning and can't fight now. He's off in the army. It's our duty to defend his family."

"I'm here to take his place," I objected.

"We know, T.J." Mr. Hill smiled. "You fight like a bobcat, too, but you couldn't hold off an Indian raid by yourself. We have to band together. I think if it's a small scouting party, we stand a pretty fair chance. But if it's a real raid, we should all come here."

"Yes," said Mr. Einsbruch. "My house is the only one with stone walls. We also have a cellar with supplies. We could stand off a full raid with our rifles from my house, knowing our women and children are safe below us."

With our plan of action settled, I mounted Cactus and headed home. I told Ma what had happened, and she smiled.

"You shouldn't have said anything to Mr. Hill," she scolded me. "I don't want you volunteering to go off and fight."

"I'll do what Pa would have done," I said.

"I know," she sighed. "I wish, though, that you were not always so stubborn about taking favors. Your pride may get you an arrow."

"I'll be careful. Besides, the Comanches are miles away."

But that wasn't the case. Just two days later, I saw smoke on the horizon. I went to the barn and saddled Cactus. Travis ran out with my rifle, and Abigail fixed a sack of food.

"Where are you going?" asked Ma.

"There's smoke," I said, pointing it out. "It's the Hill place, I'm sure. I have to go to help."

"You promised you'd only fight if the Indians came here," she complained.

"No, Ma. I won't wait for them to start scalping you or burning our house. They're here. We have to stop them now. I'm riding to the Einsbruch place. We'll get them before they get here. You get Travis and the girls and lock yourselves in the cellar. Grandma Nelson and Austin, too. Put out all the fires and shut up the pigs and the chickens. Don't come out until I get back."

"Do you know what you're doing?" she asked.

"Yes, Ma. I'll be back, too. I won't take any chances."

"Thomas," she sobbed, throwing her arms around me.

I hugged her back, wiping away a tear of my own. Then I pulled away and mounted my horse. As I rode off, I heard her barking out orders to my brothers and sisters.

3

I met up with Nels Einsbruch halfway to his place. When he saw me, he reined in his horse and waited for me to reach him.

"I was just on my way to your place," Nels called out to me. "Have you seen the smoke?"

"Is it the Hill place?" I asked Nels.

"Yes," he said. "Mr. Hill got his wife and family out just in time. They swooped down on the farm, rounding up pigs and chickens. That gave the Hills their chance. I don't think those Indians ever knew the Hills were there. Anyway, Pa and the rest of the men are getting their horses saddled back home. I rode out to get you. I thought you might be so busy with all the work you didn't have time to notice anything."

"That's about the truth." I smiled. "I never knew there was so much to be done. Travis helps some, but if I take my eye off him for a moment, he's got that fishing pole dipped into the river."

Nels turned his horse and led the way to his farm. We didn't talk as we rode, but both of us were thinking the same thing. Riding out against Indians wasn't the same thing as hunting deer. Indians could shoot back. They took scalps. They did terrible things to you if they captured you. And the worst Indians in the whole world were the Comanches.

We slowed our horses to a trot as we entered the gate of the Einsbruch farm. We could hear the sounds of children shouting and women crying. Above it all came Mr. Einsbruch's deep voice.

"Now, ladies," he said. "Get ahold of yourselves. We're riding out to meet the Indians so they won't come here. You'll be safe. We don't plan on getting killed. Tom Hill here says there's not more than fifteen Comanches. It's likely no more than a scouting party. If we can catch them, the main party may go another way."

"May God protect us," said Ned Johnson's wife.

"We must pause a minute before we leave," Mr.

Einsbruch said, growing solemn. "There may be those among us who will not return. If that is the will of God, then let us all pray now for those who will give up their lives for the protection of us all."

Nels and I bowed our heads and joined the silence.

"Dear Lord," Mr. Einsbruch said. "We ask you to look after us all in our moment of need. Ride with us that we may return sound in body and spirit. But if it is to be our time, prepare a place for us at your side. And forgive us for the lives we may take in the defense of our homes and families."

"Amen," everyone said together.

"Now, ladies," Mr. Einsbruch instructed. "Please go back to the house and enjoy the shade. We must make our plan for battle."

The women and children made their way back to the big stone house, but we could still hear the muffled sobs of the women and the high-pitched questions of the children.

"First of all," said Tom Hill, "let's get this boy a horse." He laughed, pointing to Cactus. "He'll have to have something he can keep up on."

"Nels," said Mr. Einsbruch. "Help T.J. get a horse from the barn."

Nels and I dismounted and led old Cactus to the barn.

"Cactus isn't that bad a horse," I told Nels.

"That's not why they want us over here. They're

afraid we'll get scared if we hear them talking about what they'll do for the families of the dead," Nels told me.

"What?" I asked.

"They're making plans to help the families of those who may be killed. I heard Pa talking to Hermann about it. It's only right they discuss it before, so they'll all have to lend a hand. If they waited until somebody got killed, someone could always refuse to help on the grounds no one would have helped his family."

"But we have a right to be there," I said.

"What could you do, T.J.? You have more than a grown man can do at your own place. Me, Pa always speaks for our family. It's better this way."

"You sure?"

"Yeah. Now let's pick a horse. How about this sorrel? He's a beauty, and he runs like the wind."

"You figure we'll need to run?"

"We won't be running away. But we have to catch every one of those Indians. If a single one gets away, he'll tell the others just how poorly this valley is defended."

"Then we'll do just that. There must be a thousand places to ambush Indians in this valley."

"That's what Pa's been thinking. Here's the sorrel," Nels said, leading the horse out. "You can saddle him yourself."

"Sure," I said. "Thank your pa."

"No need." Nels smiled. "If you got yourself killed,

I'd have no one to hunt deer with. Besides, Pa would have to take care of your place. And you'd be a sure target with that pretty blond hair that Bertha's always talking about."

"Nels, there's a pitchfork on this wall that would sure look good between your ears."

We laughed at each other as I saddled the horse. When I'd finished, I led the sorrel out, and we joined the others.

"That looks much better," said Ned Johnson. "'Course he'd look better with a colonel's cap and some of that buttercup braid on his sleeves."

"Leave him alone, Johnson," snapped Ken Floyd. "That boy's riding out same as you and me. And if today there's an arrow with your name on it, you'd hate to spend eternity in darkness because you bad-mouthed a boy."

"Gentlemen, please," said Mr. Einsbruch. "We must plan. In all there are twenty-three of us. We know the Comanches are likely to be at the Hill farm. They're hungry, and there is much there to eat. We wait behind the rocks by the bend of the river road. We send scouts ahead to see if they come. Understand?"

"Yes," we said together.

"Then we'll ride, but we'll go slowly, so we won't stir up dust for the whole valley to see. And when the time comes, wait for my signal to attack. One shot fired too early may cost many lives."

We rode out slowly, covering the three miles to the

Hill farm in what seemed like a hundred hours. It wasn't much more than half an hour really. Hermann Einsbruch rode ahead to check on the Indians. He returned a few minutes later, followed closely by three Comanches.

"They're coming," Hermann shouted. "All of them."

Sure enough, the whole scouting party was in hot pursuit of Hermann. I watched Mr. Einsbruch raise his hand, preparing to give the signal to fire. I raised my rifle and picked out a spot that soon would contain an Indian.

Hermann rode past his father in a hurry, and Mr. Einsbruch lowered his hand. The rocks erupted with rifle fire. Bullets whined through the air, splintering rock and bone. The first two Comanches spun to the ground, hit several times.

The Indian I fired upon was unhurt. He looked into my eyes and readied his war lance. Then he charged. When he was still twenty yards away, his head snapped back, and I watched him fall dead to the ground.

Mr. Einsbruch gave the signal to charge, and we rode down on the Comanches, firing right and left. Most of the Indians stood their ground and were killed almost instantly. Some of them returned our fire. Jed Clayburn, who was only a few years older than I was, took an arrow in the leg, and Hermann Einsbruch was shot in the head and killed.

Only two of the Comanches made a run for it. One was an old warrior. He charged into the rocks, knocking Mr. Hill from his horse. I raised my rifle in the direction of the Indian, but Ned Johnson waved me off. Then Ned spurred his horse and went after the Indian.

I thought to myself that this was true courage. But when Ned caught up with the old warrior, the Comanche turned and drove a spear into Ned's side. I saw Ned turn, his eyes suddenly lifeless and cold. Then Ned tumbled from his horse. The Comanche looked at all of us for a moment, singing a haunting death chant. Then he was cut down by a dozen rifles.

That left only one of the Indians. He was young, like me. He almost got away by riding right through the middle of us. Everyone was afraid of firing and hitting a friend. But Nels got a slug into him, and the boy fell from his horse right in front of me.

He rolled over and over, landing finally against a pile of rocks. I stepped down from my horse to see if he was dead. He was face down, a limp mass of flesh. I turned him over with my boot.

Blood was oozing out of a big hole in his side, and I saw fear in his eyes. He thought I was going to kill him. But he was very young, and even smaller than I was. I just couldn't. When Mr. Einsbruch arrived, he wanted to get it over with and kill the boy.

"They've killed my son," growled Mr. Einsbruch. "Now I'll kill one of theirs."

"Kill him for Ned," someone else shouted.

"Let T.J. do it," said a voice behind me. "It'll be something he'll be able to tell his grandchildren."

Mr. Einsbruch looked at me. But I felt no lust for killing. I only felt pity for that poor, half-naked boy. I didn't know why I should have any feeling for him at all. I knew he would probably have killed me without even thinking were he in my position. But I read in his eyes a plea for life.

"No," I said finally. "No, I won't kill him," I added, lowering my rifle.

"Then it's best done quickly," said Mr. Einsbruch. "Nels, do it."

Nels pointed his rifle at the boy's head, but I stepped in front of him.

"Can't you see he's only a boy," I said. "That could be me or Nels there. Don't you see it's not right?"

"It's necessary," Mr. Einsbruch said, leading me aside.

"No," I said. "He'll likely die of his wound. If that's to be, then it's to be. But this would be little more than murder. You can't do it."

"We can't let him go back to his people and tell them we're defenseless, boy," said Mr. Hill. "You know me, T.J., I don't find pleasure in it any more than you do. But part of war is killing your enemy."

"To defend yourself, yes," I said. "But there's no right in this. If God is watching us, he will see no good in this act. I'll take him home with me. Let him die in peace."

"You can't keep a savage penned up like a hog," John Clayburn said. "Yonder lies my brother Jed with a leg split open by those Comanches. That boy'll likely leave you with one like it. Or maybe he'll take to being liberal with your sisters. Maybe he'll scalp one of those little brothers of yours."

"Look in his eyes," I told them. "Eyes don't lie. Just as there's no courage in killing him, there's no courage in what you've said. Do those eyes speak anything but courage and honor? I'll watch him. He'll have no gun, no horse. If the time comes when he gets well and proves a danger, then I'll do what must be done. It's as easy to shoot an unarmed man one time as another."

"Boy, this is madness," said Mr. Hill.

"It's what must be," I said. "I feel there's as much justice in you killing the two of us as there is in killing him."

"Well, he'll likely never see tomorrow's sunrise," said Mr. Einsbruch, turning away. "Only I don't want to see that Comanche again. Hear me?"

"Yes, sir," I said. "He'll not leave our place."

As the others walked away to tend to their wounds or collect the Comanche horses or bury the dead, I turned to the Indian boy.

"I know you can't understand my words," I said,

"but I am a friend. Take my hand and let me help you to my home."

The fear in his eyes disappeared, and a new warmth replaced it. As I got him to his feet, he fainted, and I had to struggle to get him over the side of his horse. His blood stained my clothes, and I felt a closeness to him. Then I mounted the sorrel and led the way back home.

As we rode, I wondered why boys had to fight wars against each other. What stupidity it was for men to shoot each other. But the world was as it was, and there was little I could do about it. I already had seven people to take care of, and I had just pledged to take on another.

When I reached home, Ma ran out to greet me. As I got off the horse, she screamed. I smiled at her, then remembered the blood that was all over me.

"I'm not hurt, Ma," I said. "It's not my blood. Herman Einsbruch and Ned Johnson were killed, and one of the Clayburns was hurt, but I'm fine."

"You just get yourself down to the river and get out of those clothes," she screamed. "Travis will bring down some new things."

Then she caught sight of the second horse.

"What's that on the Indian pony?" she asked.

"It's a Comanche boy no bigger than me, Ma. He's hurt pretty bad. I brought him home to heal."

"You've got an Indian there? Alive? Child, don't

you have more sense than that? He'll get well off our food and scalp us in our sleep."

"No, Ma. There's a kindness in his eyes. I know he could never harm me, just as I couldn't harm him. I'll keep him in the barn until you trust him. I'll watch him night and day. You'll see, he'll be all right."

"You must be crazed in the head," she shouted. "Indians aren't like cattle. They think, they feel. You can't adopt him like a stray dog."

"No, Ma. But I can treat him like a man. He can understand that."

"You're taking a terrible risk. Not just for yourself, but for the rest of us, too. For the entire valley."

"I know, Ma. And if you order me to kill him, I'll do it for you. But there's no hatred in me for anything right now. And if I kill him, I'll always feel the guilt."

"Lord, boy, you do know the words that cut me deep. I'll not order you to take a life. Oh, I wish you were here, John Clinton. Boys are beyond me. You bear them, feed them, clothe them, think you've done a job educating them. Then they turn out to be unreasonable little bear cubs. Lord!"

I got the Indian boy into the river with me. As I cleaned the powder and the blood from me, I did the same for him. Travis brought clothes for me, and I told him to take Mr. Einsbruch's sorrel back and get Cactus.

"What about the Indian pony?" Travis asked.

"Take it and put it in the barn. Feed it, too."

"What you gonna do with that Indian?" my brother asked.

"Help him get well," I said.

"Then what?"

"I don't know, Travis. I purely don't know. But I think we'll know pretty soon," I added, feeling the boy's strength surging through his shoulders.

"Hope he doesn't scalp us," Travis said, heading for the barn. "Got kinda used to my hair."

"Me, too." I laughed.

4

Those first days we had the Indian boy, I began to wonder if I was so right about him. Fever burned inside his head, and twice when I wiped his forehead with wet cloths, he grabbed me around the throat. He was weak, though, and I easily squirmed loose from his grasp. Still, I wouldn't let anyone else in the barn unless I was around.

The third day he was there, the fever broke. I had him tied up while I slept, and I woke to his screams. I walked over and saw him fighting the ropes. When he saw me, he stopped struggling. He held his bound hands in front of me and whispered some words in Comanche.

I shook my head to show I didn't understand. Then I took my knife and cut the ropes. He smiled, and I held out my hand in friendship. He took it and said, *"Amigo."*

"You speak Spanish," I said. "Do you understand English?"

His blank look was my answer.

"Amigo," I repeated, pointing my finger first at myself, then at him.

"I am called T.J.," I said. "T.J.," I repeated, pointing to myself.

His eyes lit up, and he said, in his own way, "Tee Jaaay."

"Pluma Amarillo," he said then, pointing a finger at his chest.

"Amarillo means yellow," I said. *"Pluma?"* I asked, not remembering any such word.

"Pluma," he said, taking my hand and drawing in the dirt of the barn floor.

When he finished, I saw that he meant feather. "Yellow Feather," I said, pointing to him. "In my language, Pluma Amarillo means Yellow Feather."

"Yellow Feather," he repeated, pointing my fingers at his bare chest.

"Yes," I said. "I wish you spoke English. I only know a little Spanish. We had a man named Miguel who worked for Pa. He was Mexican, and he spoke Spanish. I wish I'd learned more."

"Tee Jaaay," he said, shaking his head. "Amigos," he said then, smiling.

Looking into his eyes again, I knew I had nothing to fear from him.

By the end of the week, he was on his feet again. His clothes were badly torn by his fall, and he ran naked around the barn. Now that he was ready to leave the barn, I had a problem. I didn't know how to explain to him that he couldn't walk around naked and let my sisters see him.

Finally, I took some of my old trousers and a shirt and handed them to him. I showed him how to put them on, and he started to put them on—on me. I laughed and shook my head. I didn't know how to tell him they were for him. I didn't have the right words.

Then by accident the problem was solved. Yellow Feather was helping me move some tools around in the barn. I had a deerskin stretching on the wall, hoping I'd have time to fashion some buckskin trousers. Yellow Feather took the deerskin off the wall and wrapped it around his waist.

"Yo uso?" he asked, his eyes telling me that he wanted the hide to make some clothes.

"For you." I smiled, handing it back to him as he gave it to me. "You'll never know how relieved I am for you to have it." I sighed.

The next gift was far more difficult. He asked for a

knife. I knew he had to have a knife to cut the deerskin, but knives were for other things, too. I knew that only danger would come of my not trusting him, though. As long as we were friends, brothers, I had nothing to fear from him.

By the next morning he'd made deerskin leggings, vest, and breechcloth for himself. He'd also made a vest for me, which he handed me proudly, along with my knife. Now that I knew I could trust him with the knife, I returned it to him. He smiled, then threw the knife like a bullet into the side of the barn. I knew he understood it would make my family nervous if he wore it. In the barn, it would be available whenever he needed it.

We worked hard those next few weeks. Winter was not far off, and there was much to be done. We gathered grass in bundles for the stock, fixed fences that had fallen, replaced shingles a windstorm had dislodged, and minded the cattle.

Yellow Feather would sometimes strike up a conversation in Spanish with me, and I would do the same in English. Neither of us understood any but a few of the words, but there was a feeling that was shared, and that was enough.

Yellow Feather also sang Comanche songs. They were sad, mournful, and the look in his eyes when he finished told me he missed his home. I had learned from him that his father had been one of the warriors in the scouting party who had been killed. His mother had died in childbirth. He had no family, so I guess he had adopted mine.

Ma was always nervous around him, but he was never less than polite, and she had gotten to the point of almost tolerating him. The girls were deathly afraid and would scream if he even approached them.

Travis and Austin, on the other hand, were just the opposite. They loved to ride around on his back, and Travis learned all sorts of clever fishing tricks from Yellow Feather.

As for the work, having Yellow Feather around was like having a second me. No matter how I tried, he always made sure he did more than I did. He never seemed to tire.

Then one day in late September one of the steers stepped into a hole and had to be shot. We stripped the hide, and Ma started cooking the meat. We would eat steaks and salt the rest for use later. I wanted to take the hide to Mr. Einsbruch, though, to use for my new boots.

I didn't know what to do. Mr. Einsbruch would shoot Yellow Feather if I took him with me. And Ma would have a fit if I left him alone on the farm. Finally, I saddled old Cactus and turned to took at him.

"I have to take the hide to another rancho," I said. "I go *rancho grande*."

Yellow Feather pointed to his horse and showed me with his hands that he wanted to go, too.

"No," I said sadly. "You can't go."

Yellow Feather's eyes filled with sadness. He looked away from me. Then he walked over to the stall he slept in and picked up a rope. He held it out for me to tie him with.

"I can't," I said, shaking my head.

"*Por* Ma and Travis," he said, mixing the English and Spanish as he always did now.

"Yes," I said. "For them."

After tying him, I rode off to the Einsbruch place with the hide. Arriving there, I tied up my horse and went to the front door.

"Why, look," said Mrs. Einsbruch. "It's T.J. Clinton. Bertha will be glad to see you, young man," she told me. "We haven't seen you since the Comanche raid."

"Yes, ma'am," I said. "Don't tell Bertha. I came to ask Mr. Einsbruch for his help in curing a hide. I want to use the leather for some boots."

"He's in the barn," she told me. "Nels is there, too. Hermann would be too if those Indians had not killed him. Savages!"

"I'm sorry," I said.

"Was nothing you did." She smiled at me. "Life here is hard. If not the Indians, then the war. If not the heat, then the cold."

"Yes." I frowned, turning toward the barn.

When I got there, Nels ran out to greet me.

"Hey, stranger. Where you been? It's hunting

season, and I haven't seen sign of you. When are we going to go for some deer?"

"I've been busy with the farm, Nels," I explained. "There's so much to be done. If I leave the farm, then there's no one there. You understand."

"Yes," he said. "What can we do for you today?"

"I hoped I might talk to your pa about getting some help tanning this hide," I said, pointing to the cowhide on the back of my horse.

"Sure. Nothing to it. Pa, T.J.'s here. He wants some help curing a hide."

"Good to see you, boy," Mr. Einsbruch said. "I didn't figure we'd see you until that Comanche boy finally died. It took this long?"

"No, sir," I said. "It didn't. Fact is, he didn't die at all. You wouldn't believe how much help he's been on the farm."

"He's not with you?" asked Mr. Einsbruch, reaching for a rifle.

"No, sir. You told me I wasn't to let him get near here."

"Then where?" asked Nels.

"At home," I said.

"You'd leave an Indian all alone at your place? Why, he's probably scalped your whole family by now."

"No, sir," I said. "He wouldn't. Anyway, he's all tied up."

"I get it." Nels laughed. "Pa, he's put one over on

us. He's using that Indian as a slave. That T.J.'s no fool. All this time we took him for an Indian lover, and he's really just a good businessman. He knew he'd have a time of it keeping the farm going, so he picked himself up an inexpensive slave."

They shared each other's laughter, but I kept my own thoughts to myself. I had a father and two brothers fighting for the South, but we were opposed to slavery. Pa always said a man should live or die by the work he could do with his own two hands.

Mr. Einsbruch got the curing process started, promising to send Nels over with the hide when it was ready. I laughed at the thought of having Nels discover Yellow Feather was more like a brother to me than a slave.

As I was leaving, Nels promised to come by in a day or so to go hunting for deer. For him it was sport. For me, it was part of making it through the winter. Deer meat and buckskin clothes would go a long way toward keeping our small herd of cattle intact.

When I got home, Yellow Feather was waiting for me in his stall. I untied the ropes, and he smiled. Travis had sat beside him the whole time.

As I went to sleep that night, I thanked God that I had found a friend like Yellow Feather.

5

The rest of September raced by. Soon October, too, had passed. November brought chill winds and an early snow. It also brought our second raid of the year, a raid of a different kind.

I was making the morning rounds when I found that two of our chickens were missing. I found some feathers and bloodstained leaves, but no signs of the chickens. Concerned, I decided to track the thief.

I managed to walk over about half a mile of rocky ground before I found some soft sand with tracks. They were clear, but frightening. I'd seen enough wolf tracks to recognize that was what they were, but

I'd never seen any wolf print near approaching the size of these.

Bending down beside them, I put my hand on one of the prints. Then I put my foot beside it. Counting the claws, the paw was bigger than either. I couldn't escape the terrible feeling that the wolf was just over the next hill watching me, thinking to itself what a tasty morsel I would be.

My courage suddenly vanished. I was no longer a brave young man guarding his family against all enemies. I was more than ever before a frightened boy up against he knew not what. I made my way through the brush and the prickly pear back to the house, imagining there were eyes on me the whole time. Every rush of the wind seemed like the wolf clawing at my back.

When I reached the house, I tried to catch my breath as I went inside.

"Thomas," Ma said. "Did you know something got into the chicken coop last night? Two hens are missing."

"Ma," I said. "Keep the girls and Austin inside until I get back."

"What's the matter?" asked Travis.

"Travis, do you think you can fire Pa's rifle?" I asked.

"Sure," my brother answered. "We going deer hunting?"

"We're not going out to hunt anything right now," I

said. "But I'm not sure there isn't something out there hunting us."

"What?" asked Hope. "You mean there's something out there?"

"Sure," grinned Travis. "It's had a nice breakfast of chicken. Now it's ready for lunch. It'd like a nice plump girl."

"Travis, come here," I said, leading my little brother outside.

"Yeah?" he asked.

"Travis, you're almost eleven years old. I wish you were older or stronger or something, but you're all I've got. There's a wolf out there bigger than the two of us put together. Those girls are going to be scared enough. I need your help. You've got to be brave and strong. Now I'm going to tell Yellow Feather. You keep everybody inside."

"Hey, you're serious, aren't you?" Travis asked.

I looked into his big brown eyes and noticed they were older than I'd remembered. There was something a little more solid about his shoulders, too, and I smiled at him.

"Travis, you're growing up. It ought to take more time than one night, but there just isn't any more time sometimes. That wolf is going to be a lot tougher than any Comanche Indian. It's going to be mean and hungry. Whatever you do, don't try anything by yourself. You just keep inside. If it comes around, you give it a blast with that rifle."

45

"Sure, T.J. Be careful, huh?" Travis said, putting his little hand on my arm.

"You, too," I said, patting him on the back.

Yellow Feather was busy spreading hay for the horses when I walked into the barn. He looked up at me and his smile vanished.

"You worry," he said, using one of the English phrases he'd picked up from my conversations with Ma.

"Yes," I said. "Yellow Feather, come here," I told him, sitting down on the floor of the barn.

Yellow Feather put aside the pitchfork and sat beside me.

"There is a wolf, a *lobo*," I began, looking deep into his eyes. "It is raiding. It killed chickens last night."

"Lobo," he said, frowning. "Comanche kill *muchos lobos*. Kill with rifle, bow, knife. I kill lobo five moon past. Chief very proud. Let Yellow Feather go raid with Father."

When he said this, the fire within his eyes died, and we shared his sadness in silence.

"This is a big lobo," I said.

"Big?" Yellow Feather asked, stretching his arms out as a measure of its size.

"I don't know. I didn't see. Its paws are huge," I said, pointing to my hand. "I'll show you."

I drew in the dirt floor the size of the paw around my hand. As I drew, Yellow Feather laughed.

"Ojos grandes," he said.

46

"I know what you mean," I said. "You think my eyes are too big. You think I'm making this up."

I scratched out the paw print and drew it a second time, the same size.

"*Sí?*" he asked, looking into my eyes. "This so?"

"Yes," I sighed. *"Lobo grande."*

"*Sí,*" said Yellow Feather, standing up. "No see?"

"No," I answered, shaking my head.

"Take me," he said, pointing to the paw print I'd drawn on the floor.

"Yes," I said, leading the way.

Before going, I stopped and took a rifle out of Pa's gun cabinet. Before, I'd always carried my deer rifle. Now, I took one of the long hunting rifles Pa had brought back from Houston City five years before.

Yellow Feather's eyes told me he wanted to carry a rifle, too, but we both knew it wasn't possible.

When we reached the soft sand, Yellow Feather got down on his knees and peered at the print. He looked all around at the others, then frowned.

Shaking his head, he said, "This *lobo* very *grande.*"

Then he bared his teeth and snarled to show me he knew it was mean, too. Just then we heard a stirring in the brush, and a low growl sounded in our ears.

I tried to keep from trembling as I brought the rifle around to bear on the sound. But the sound wasn't coming from any one place. It was everywhere at once. We made our way quickly back to the farm.

Once home, we exchanged looks which said everything. There was an enemy out there ready to kill us. We had to be ready. When it struck, death for us or the beast must follow.

I walked around the farmyard, carefully listening for sounds. I sent Travis and Yellow Feather down to bring the cattle up to the barn. I wasn't eager to have them stay in the barn with Yellow Feather, but that wolf could kill them all in one night's work.

As evening closed around us, I grew nervous. After dinner I nailed the shutters closed and went inside the house.

"Ma, I want you all to stay back. Travis knows how to fire a rifle, so he can keep the wolf at bay. If it gets through the door, head for the cellar."

"What about Travis?" asked little Austin.

"I'll be fighting the wolf," Travis said nervously.

I looked at him with pride. We both knew that if the wolf got in, Travis would be dead.

As I took two rifles from the gun closet, Travis reached out his hand and wrapped his arm around my side. There was a single tear in his eye.

"I wish there was more time for us to talk like we used to, Travis," I told him. "There are so many things I want to tell you about life. But there's never any time."

"I know, T.J.," he said. "You know I'll do my best."

"If Yellow Feather and I do our job, that old wolf won't bother you at all. If it should," I began, swallowing deeply, "if something happens to me, get

48

the girls, Ma, Austin, and Grandma and head for the Einsbruch place. They'll be glad to help all they can."

"T.J., I'm scared," Travis said, burying his face in my side.

"I know," I told him. "But it's got to be done. And I'm really counting on you this time. You know you really are lazy. You spend all your time fishing when you should be working. I don't know if you'll ever make a farmer."

"Yeah." He smiled, wiping his eyes with his shirt sleeve. "I'll do better."

"You'd better."

"See you in the morning, T.J."

"Not before," I said sternly. "No matter what you hear, stay inside and keep this door bolted."

"Who's the second gun for?" Ma asked as I went outside.

"For Yellow Feather," I mumbled.

"You can't do that, T.J. Once that boy gets a gun, he'll be a Comanche warrior. You won't have just one enemy out there. You'll have two."

"Ma, you know he's had his chances."

"I know he wouldn't scalp us. He likes us. But he might just decide to take his horse and scamper once he has a gun."

"He's little help against a wolf with his bare hands!" I yelled. "If he runs off, we're no worse off. And if he stays, he might just save all our lives."

We picked a hill overlooking the barnyard to wait

for the wolf. That also put us in a position to cover any attack on the house or barn. I handed Yellow Feather the rifle and watched his eyes. They grew wide, and he clasped my hand.

"*Amigos,*" he smiled. "*Amigos grandes.*"

We waited for the wolf. The moonlight shed its light over the barnyard, lending a haunting glow to everything. Even the chickens and the hogs seemed bewitched. Then we heard a low growl, and we swung our rifles to bear.

In an instant, the wolf was there, ripping the gate of the chicken coop apart. I aimed carefully and fired the rifle. The bullet exploded against the side of the wolf, but nothing happened. The beast turned to stare at me, its terrifying red eyes sending a shiver down my spine. Its hide blazed bright silver, almost ghostlike, in the moonlight. Then it grabbed a chicken in its jaws, growled, and disappeared into the night.

6

I couldn't get out of my mind the picture of that wolf, its red eyes glaring at me. I saw it through the sights of my rifle, and it had been barely twenty yards away. My hands hadn't been shaking. The rifle had been steady. And yet it was as if I hadn't fired the gun at all.

When morning came, I walked back down the hill to face my family. Travis was asleep at his post, the rifle, which was too big for him, resting on the kitchen table that braced the front door.

"Good morning," I shouted to Travis.

"Huh?" he asked sleepily. "Is that you, T.J.?"

"Me and Yellow Feather," I said, feeling the Indian boy at my side. "Is everybody all right?"

"Sure," grinned Travis. "I did just what you said. I guarded the house all night. I fell asleep when it got light, but I would have wakened up if that wolf had come back. Did you kill him, T.J.?"

"I think I hit him," I said. "It's all strange. I had my sights dead center on him. I pulled the trigger, but it was as if the bullet flew right through that wolf. It just snarled at me and went on its way, taking another chicken with it."

Yellow Feather handed me the rifle I'd given him, and I put it back in the gun cabinet. As the Indian left, Ma grabbed my arm.

"Thomas, you are very lucky that boy is still here," she said.

"Yes, Ma. It's good to know I'm not fighting this thing all alone."

"But will he stand by you? You said yourself this is no ordinary creature. Can you trust him to save your life?"

"I guess, Ma, I won't know that until the time comes. But there's something about the way Yellow Feather acted last night that makes me think there's more to this wolf than big feet and red eyes."

"You think it's a Comanche trick?"

"No," I said. "We have little of value to the Comanches. Old Cactus wouldn't carry a sick dog anywhere the Comanches go. If they took us captive, it would touch off another war. No, the Comanches aren't pulling a trick."

As I walked out to the barn to join Yellow Feather, I tried to consider Ma's warning. But the words carried no weight. Sure, they were true enough. Comanches were ruthless. I had no doubt a Comanche was capable of taking my life.

But what my heart told me about Yellow Feather was more important. He could never harm us. We were as much a family to him as he knew. And yet there was something he wasn't telling me about that wolf. I could read in his eyes something terrible, something frightening.

Yellow Feather was standing by his horse's stall, gently stroking the pony with the kind of love a boy has for his only real friend. I walked up behind him and sat down on the straw floor.

"Amigo," I called to him.

Yellow Feather turned and looked at me, his usual smile missing. There were wrinkles on his forehead, and his eyes were full of the fear I had seen when I stood over his bleeding body after the ambush.

"There is something wrong?" I asked him.

"*Sí*," he said, sitting down beside me. "Wrong. Much wrong."

I sat silently, waiting for him to tell me.

"Lobo is no lobo," he said sadly.

"The wolf isn't a wolf?" I asked. "Then what is it?"

"Is *Diablo Argentino*," he said, terror in his eyes.

"Devil," I translated. "Silver devil. The wolf is a devil?"

"Lobo is spirit. Comanche tell of Diablo Argentino. Is very bad spirit. Do evil to man."

"Come on, Yellow Feather." I smiled. "You don't believe that?"

"Yellow Feather believe now," he told me. "You think you kill lobo last night. *Sí?*"

"Yes," I said. "I shot him square."

"There no blood," Yellow Feather said. "Silver devil can never be killed by bullet or knife."

"According to legend, perhaps," I said. "But any real animal can be killed."

Yellow Feather looked at me for a moment, trying to understand my words. Then he smiled.

"Is way silver devil be killed. I tell you."

"Go on," I told him.

"Many summers ago, in land of Comanche, devil spirit grow angry with Indian. Say Indian no longer brave, no longer strong. Many men no longer hunt in way of fathers. So devil spirit come to earth as lobo. Great lobo with silver hair and eyes of fire."

"Red eyes," I said.

"*Sí*, eyes of fire. Diablo seek to test Comanches. He come to test strength, courage, truth of heart. No bullet harm him. No arrow draw blood. Only courage and honor can drive away."

"I like the story," I said. "But things don't really happen that way. This devil spirit or wolf or lobo or whatever it is isn't going to run away just because we show courage."

"More than courage," Yellow Feather said, his eyes telling me this was the part he feared most. "Only two young warriors with heart pure and brave can kill lobo. It said that lobo come to test bond between them. If one weak, both die. But if both strong, then lobo die."

"So it takes two young warriors with pure hearts to kill it. That's you and me, Yellow Feather. Even if your legend is true, we can kill the wolf."

"Hearts not pure," Yellow Feather said, pointing to both of us. "Bullet not kill. We die," he said and his eyes told me he believed it.

"No," I said. "We will live, you and I. We will prove our courage."

He looked into my eyes and read my thoughts. The fear left his face, and he took my hand.

"Amigos," he said, pointing first to himself and then to me. *Amigos valientes.*

"Yes," I said wearily. "I'll sleep for a couple of hours. Then I must go tell the others in the valley." I signaled with my hand that I was going to the house.

When I went to get Cactus a few hours later, Yellow Feather walked over and took out the rope. I wanted to ignore it, but he reached out and touched my arm. With his eyes he told me my duty, and I tied him. Then I saddled old Cactus and rode out.

There was really just one place I had to go, the

Einsbruch farm. Once Mr. Einsbruch was alerted, he'd spread the word to the others. If I went to each farm myself, our place would be defenseless too long.

Cactus trotted along the dusty road, and I was thankful the weather had cooled. All around me the trees were shedding their scrubby leaves. Only the live oaks kept their leaves through winter.

Up ahead, a big white oak stood ghostlike at the bend in the road, and I shivered at the sight. When I was little, we used to believe that tree was haunted. Now it only reminded me that I was a boy no more.

I thought about many things on the way to the Einsbruchs' place. I thought about Pa and my brothers. I wondered if they were all right. We never got word of the war. For all we knew, it might be over by now. But if it was, we didn't know if it had been won or lost.

I wondered, too, if Ma had been right about Yellow Feather. Would he really run off one night? My heart told me no, but my experience with Indians was limited. I knew that in his place, I'd hardly risk my life for an enemy.

Most of all, I wondered about myself. Did I have within me the courage to stand up to the devil beast? I wasn't sure about all that legend talk, but I did know I'd have to have plenty of courage to kill such a huge animal.

And there was the other thing, which I tried not to think about at all. Death. What did it mean to die?

Would it hurt to be clawed and torn by the devil beast? Would death just be a long dream, as Pa had told me when Grandpa Clinton had died?

Before I could wonder anymore, I found myself approaching the gate to the Einsbruch farm. I sat up in the saddle, eager to make a good impression. I watched as Nels raced out to open the gate for me.

"Hey, T.J.," he called to me. "Where've you been keeping yourself? Hunting season's just about gone."

"I've been hunting something else," I told him. "We've got a wolf on the prowl over at my place."

"Timber wolf?" asked Mr. Einsbruch, charging out of the barn. "You got timber wolves on your farm?"

"No, sir," I said. "Just one wolf, if you can believe it's really a wolf."

"What you talking about, boy?" asked Mr. Einsbruch. "Let's get in the house and get us some lemonade. I think you must have too much sun on your head to talk in such a way."

"What did you mean out there?" asked Nels as we walked inside. "What else could it be?"

"It's not like anything I've ever seen," I told him. "Its paws are twice the size of any I've seen before, and Pa and Jackson shot a wolf once that had a fifty-dollar bounty on its head."

"I remember that wolf," Mr. Einsbruch said, handing me a cold glass of lemonade. "You say this wolf is bigger?"

"Twice easy," I said, sipping the drink. "And there's

57

something weird about it. Its hide is silver. It's like a ghost the way it suddenly appears right on top of you."

"You ever seen a ghost, T.J.?" Nels asked, laughing.

"I've seen this thing, Nels. And there're the eyes. Those eyes are full of fire. I've never seen an animal with eyes like that. They seem to be looking right through you. They seem to reach down into your heart and search it. I've never come up against anything like it."

"You've got your imagination all stirred up," Nels told me. "You've been out there with all those girls too long. We'll just round up some men and go out and kill it. Shoot, there's probably a big bounty on a wolf that size."

"It's not going to be easy," I said. "I wasn't twenty yards away and hit it square with a rifle. It didn't even shake. It just glared at me and snatched up a chicken."

"You must have been excited," Mr. Einsbruch said. "You missed."

"Nels," I said. "You ever know me to miss a target moving or still from twenty yards?"

"Can't say I have. And we shot a bobcat and a cougar last fall up that draw by Buffalo Creek."

"I'm not making all this up," I said. "There's a story about it, too."

"A story?" asked Nels.

"Yellow Feather told me. According to Comanche

legend, their devil spirit comes to earth in the form of a wolf. It tests the courage of warriors. If there are two young men with true hearts, then they can kill the beast, and the spirit will go away. But if they are false, then they will die."

"And those young men would be you and the Indian, right?" asked Mr. Einsbruch.

"I suppose," I said.

"Boy, that Indian's talking you into giving him a gun. Once he gets that gun, he'll be raiding the farms and causing more grief than any ten wolves."

"He's had his chances to run off," I said. "If he does, I'm no worse off then if he was dead. I don't know if I'd have made it into winter without his help with the cattle. And we'd never have got in all the hay if he hadn't helped."

"I'd have come out and helped you," Nels said.

"I know," I said. "But you know I couldn't have asked you. Pa wouldn't have wanted help from neighbors. It's my job to get it done."

"Your pa wouldn't have wanted an Indian around your place, either," Mr. Einsbruch said.

"He'd have understood. Thank you for the lemonade," I said, taking my hat and standing up. "Please pass on the word about the wolf to the others."

"You mean about the devil?" asked Nels.

"Whatever it is, believe this," I said. "It is big enough to kill anyone or anything. And it will take great courage to stand up to it."

"Be careful," said Mr. Einsbruch as I left. "Not just with the wolf, either."

"I'll be careful," I said. "I have to be."

"Good," Mr. Einsbruch said.

As I mounted Cactus, I found myself feeling very alone. I wasn't really part of the Einsbruchs' world as I used to be. I wasn't part of Yellow Feather's world, either. I was alone, strangely trapped somewhere in between.

7

It was late afternoon when I finally led old Cactus through the gate of our farm. I was tired and hungry, but I went first to the barn.

Yellow Feather was as I'd left him, sitting quietly next to the post where he was tied. I left Cactus standing by the door and went over to the Indian boy.

"I've returned," I said to him.

Yellow Feather stood and held out his hands for me to untie. When I'd loosened the ropes, I set to work on his feet while he wriggled his arms free. When we were finished, I walked over to Cactus.

"I take," Yellow Feather told me, taking the reins

from me. "I have great hunger," he said, smiling, knowing I was probably hungry, too.

Leaving him to tend to my horse, I raced to the house to get us some lunch. Ma shook her head as I walked in. Then she led me to the cupboard.

"Thomas, you've got to slow down some. You look like you've just run all the way up from the Gulf of Mexico."

"No, Ma. I just ran from the barn. I did have to walk some of the way back from the Einsbruchs' place. Poor old Cactus is getting old. I'm afraid he won't make too many more winters."

"We're all of us getting old," Ma said. "Some of us get better as we get older."

"Like you," I said, hugging her. "You and your cooking."

"Here, Thomas. You take this bread and dried beef and eat good. Feed that Indian, too. You two may have another long night."

"I'm afraid so, Ma. That wolf won't be satisfied with one scrawny chicken. He might decide he'd like to tackle a scrawny boy like me for dinner tonight."

"Hush, Thomas. The little ones will start getting all jittery again if you keep this up."

"Okay, Ma. Thanks for the lunch."

I left the house and walked slowly into the barn. Yellow Feather was brushing old Cactus with the same love he always showed for the little Indian pony. Yellow Feather was good with animals, and I think it was the kind of work he liked best of all. I chuckled as I thought that that was probably why he was so good with Travis, too.

"Food," I said, munching some dried beef as Yellow Feather turned my way.

"Good," he said, walking over to me and holding out his hands.

"Take this," I said, breaking the bread in two pieces and handing him one. "Here," I added, giving him a chunk of dried beef.

We ate our simple meal in silence. Then I motioned for him to follow me outside.

"Let's get some bait for the wolf," I said. "Besides, I could sure use some new clothes. We haven't been down to the deer thicket, and it should be crawling with bucks by now."

"We hunt deer," Yellow Feather said. "Get meat for wolf. Make new clothes. Soon moon of great ice come."

"Yes," I said. "Winter will be here soon. We'll have to be ready."

I was glad we were going hunting. It would also give me a chance for some target practice. More than that, it would take my mind off the coming night and what would happen when the wolf returned.

After taking the rifles from the gun closet, we walked to the thicket together. I hummed an old song my grandfather had taught me, and Yellow Feather hummed a song his grandfather might have taught him. We were singing songs from two different worlds, but I felt very close to him. I don't think there was very much difference between us at that moment.

The deer thicket was crowded with deer, and I killed a big buck with my second shot. It was a clean kill, right through the heart, and Yellow Feather praised my shooting.

We dragged the buck back down the road, and I wished we'd brought one of the horses. Yellow Feather and I were used to hard work, though, and we got the deer back to the farm before suppertime.

There was a rack behind the barn for dressing meat, and I led the way. Yellow Feather started off the process by cutting off the head and cleaning out the entrails. I started the skinning. We took time for a dinner of venison steaks. Then we returned to the job of smoking the meat.

When we finally finished the deer, Yellow Feather put the skin on the stretching rack, and I took what was left of the carcass out to the edge of the woods. I hoped the wolf would prefer that for its dinner and leave the chicken coop alone. We then stretched out alongside each other in the barn and slept.

When we awoke, darkness had settled in. A feeling of uneasiness came over me, and I went in the house. I opened the gun closet and took out the rifles once again. I handed the smallest one to Travis and took two others out for Yellow Feather and me. I patted Travis on the back and listened outside as he slid the bolt into place. Then I met Yellow Feather at the barn.

"It will come for us tonight," I said. "The wolf will be ready to kill. We must be brave and true of heart."

Yellow Feather caught my words, smiling at the thought that I'd remembered his tale of the Comanche devil beast. He took the rifle I handed him and followed me up the hill.

"Lobo come soon," he said as we reached the top.

"Yes," I said. "It has no fear of us. We will fight it."

We sat silently together for several minutes. Then Yellow Feather stirred. He lay down flat on the ground, cradling the rifle under his ribs.

"Tee Jay," he whispered. "Put gun like me."

I watched as he showed me how to cover the gun with my body. Then Yellow Feather pushed his gun in front of him. Lying so close to the ground, he was nearly invisible.

"Comanche way," he told me softly. "You do same."

I matched his posture, noticing that even my shadow was hidden in the moonlight. The wolf would have a tough time seeing us.

The wind whistled out of the north, sending a shiver of cold down my spine. I shook myself deeper into the coat my father had left behind, wishing I had one for Yellow Feather. He wore only a deerskin vest over his shoulders, and he shivered with cold.

I shook myself out of my numbness to watch the ground in front of us. I wondered if the wolf would come. I wondered if I could kill it. I wondered if I could face death bravely if the wolf killed me. But all those thoughts left my mind as I dreamed of morning and the comfortable warmth of my bed.

Twice I almost fell asleep. Both times I was rattled awake by the harsh cry of a screech owl. I turned to Yellow Feather, but his eyes had a fire in them that was meant for our enemy, the devil spirit, the wolf.

I found myself watching the stars change. With each passing hour, I grew more nervous. What if the wolf came from the woods behind us? Would I be quick enough to turn and fire in time? Would Yellow Feather stay and help me or run away to rejoin his people, as Ma had said?

I didn't have any answers, only more questions. Then I heard a growl from the direction of the barn, and everything else was forgotten.

Yellow Feather heard it, too, for he swung his rifle in that very direction. Soon a flash of silver broke through my sights, and I saw those fiery red eyes glaring at me. I rested the rifle in my eager hands and aimed. Then I fired.

The wolf dodged the bullet, but then Yellow Feather fired. The wolf growled, and the bullet slammed home Still there was no blood, though, and the wolf ran over to the deer carcass, grabbed it in his teeth, and hauled it away into the woods.

"It's gone," I said. "You hit it, but it just ran away."

Yellow Feather said nothing. He walked to the base of the hill and looked at the spot where the wolf had been hit. There wasn't a drop of blood, and Yellow Feather sank to his knees.

He chanted to his spirits for several minutes. Then he calmly stood up and walked back to the top of the hill.

"It's no use," I shouted to him. "It won't be back tonight. There's too much food to be eaten."

I saw the glint of his rifle, though, and I walked back up the hill and rejoined him. I wanted to run inside and sink into the warm comforts that waited for me there. But it was not to be, and instead I felt the chill of the night air as we waited for the wolf's return.

The great devil beast had finished with us that night, though. It didn't return, and dawn brought a strange peace to me. I fell asleep on the hill, dreaming of battlefields a thousand miles away. It seemed to take my mind off the dangers before me, and I was content.

8

It was a morning breeze that stirred me from my slumber. A heavy fog hung in the air, and I coughed myself awake. A shudder wound through me, and I struggled to my feet.

My first thought was that Yellow Feather must be frozen. When I turned to face him, though, I discovered he was gone.

"You're no stupid Comanche," I told the air. "You've gone to the barn were there's some warmth. You didn't stay out here and freeze like your fool of a friend."

I shouldered my rifle after unloading it. Then I

walked down to the barn. As I entered the barnyard, Travis came flying out to me.

"I'm sure glad to see you, T.J.," he said, hugging me. "I thought I saw the wolf drag something off with it last night. Then when Yellow Feather came down this morning all alone, I thought for sure you were eaten up."

"Not a chance," I said, yawning. "No wolf's got the best of me yet."

"Where's Yellow Feather?" Travis asked.

"In the barn, I suppose," I answered.

"No," Travis told me. "He rode off on that little pony about an hour ago."

"What!" I exclaimed.

"Yeah," Travis said. "His face was white as a sheet. I thought you must have been killed."

I ran to the barn to check what Travis had said. Sure enough, there was no sign of Yellow Feather or the Indian pony. Worse, there was not a sign of the rifle I'd handed him the night before. He was gone, mounted and armed. Yellow Feather, my sworn friend, was once again a feared Comanche warrior.

In all the time Ma had warned me Yellow Feather would one day run off, I never for a second imagined he really would. It wasn't that I didn't understand. He was alone in a world of his enemies. He couldn't even speak with them very well. At any moment, some white man could shoot him without any harm coming to the killer as a result.

Then there was the wolf. Yellow Feather had been stricken with fear ever since the wolf had first appeared. We were both afraid, but to me it was just a wolf. To Yellow Feather, that wolf was the devil itself.

"Is he gone for good?" asked Travis.

"I think so," I sighed.

"I'll miss him. He was my friend. And he sure had a way with horses."

"Yes," I smiled. "And now I'm really alone."

"You still have me," Travis said, poking his head up next to my side. "I'm getting bigger every day."

"You've been a big help," I said, running my fingers through his soft, fine hair. "But Yellow Feather was more like a man. He knew how to do so many things. I learned from him."

"I know," Travis said. "He taught me a lot about fishing. He was a good man. But now we'll be better friends."

"Yes," I said. "I've been neglecting your upbringing. Just now you need a bath," I said, picking him up and carrying him out back to the big wooden tub we used for that purpose.

"Hey, wait," yelled Travis. "I swam last week in the river. I don't need a bath."

"Sure, you do," I said, laughing as I set him down. "You want to strip or go in fully clothed?"

"I'll strip." He sighed, walking over behind a big live oak tree. "You better put the water in, though.

I don't think I could force myself to work that hard to take a bath."

I laughed at him the way I used to laugh at things. I surprised myself, for I really was upset at Yellow Feather's leaving. But in many ways, I had less responsibility now. I hurried down to the river, brought up two buckets of water and dumped them in the tub.

"Okay, Travis," I called to him.

"I'm ready," he called back, tiptoeing his way over to the tub and falling in.

"It's cold!" he yelled, popping back out.

"Take the soap," I told him, tossing a brick of hard lye soap to him. "Get off all the smell and all the dirt."

"I will," Travis frowned. "You have to go next, though."

"You fix the water, and I'll be over after breakfast," I told my brother.

"All right," Travis moaned. "Work, work, work, and more work!"

I smiled as I walked back to the house. Opening the door, I saw Ma and the girls already collected around the table.

"We've been waiting for you," Hope said. "Travis and Austin have already eaten. We want you to tell us how you killed the wolf."

"I didn't kill it," I said. "There's something else," I said, turning to Ma. "Ma, Yellow Feather took his pony and the gun I handed him last night and left. I suppose he's gone back to his people."

"Thank God," Ma said. "Now this whole valley can relax. That boy was never any trouble for us, but he would have been. Sooner or later someone would have come up here to kill him. Then you'd have had a mighty hard decision, Thomas. I'm not sure you could have given that boy up."

"I couldn't have, Ma. It's hard to believe he's gone. It'll be hard to get through the winter without him."

After breakfast, Ma found me sitting alone beside the front window.

"I saw you and Travis this morning," she said. "You'll get to know each other again now. You know, I couldn't have got him into that tub without a shotgun. He follows you like a duck follows his ma."

"I know," I said. "He's getting that tub ready for me right now. I know Travis and I are close, but Yellow Feather was someone who could help out in a fight. I don't know how this thing with the wolf's going to come out, but I'm sure of this: No one man's going to fight that thing and come out of it in one piece."

"You'll have help. The whole valley's going to have to fight a wolf that size," Ma told me.

"No, Ma. I saw that wolf. It was looking right through me as if I wasn't there at all. No, Ma. That wolf'll come here to battle me. Me alone. It's my Veracruz, and if I'm lucky, I'll get out of it okay."

"Don't think of it any other way," Ma told me. "I pray you'll be all right."

"And I pray Pa will be back before spring," I said. "I can't get the planting done alone. Without a crop next year, we won't make it."

"Sure we will," Ma scolded me. "We have the river. We can fish. There are berries and cattails and prickly pears. People used to live here before they ever heard of corn or cows."

I nodded my head. Then I heard a loud scream from Travis. I ran outside to see what was happening.

"What's wrong?" I asked.

"It's cold," Travis yelled, wrapping himself in his shirt. "Get me a towel so I can dry myself. If you don't pretty soon, I'll be frozen."

"Sure," I laughed. "You know you've got pretty legs," I told him. "If Amy Prentiss could see you now! Wow!"

"You say anything else, and I'll go get that Bertha Einsbruch to come scrub your back. She'd love to do that. She gets all giggly whenever anyone mentions your name."

"Okay," I laughed. "We're even. You get dry and get my water ready," I added, tossing him a towel.

"Yes, sir, Captain Clinton," Travis said, saluting. "Right away, sir," he added, trying to muster the deepest voice he could.

When I'd scrubbed half my hide off with the lye

soap, I took a towel and began drying off. The wind cut through my bare back, and I winced. I couldn't get my clothes on fast enough.

That afternoon as I was working in the barnyard, Nels Einsbruch and his father rode up.

"Hello, there," said Mr. Einsbruch. "Heard your Indian hired help hightailed it back across the Red River."

"Who'd you hear that from?" I asked.

"Pete Simpson. He said that boy rode like wildfire across his place about an hour ago. Pete said that Indian could have scalped half the valley, but the boy doesn't seem to have a heart for killing. Just wanted to get away."

"I'm glad no one was troubled," I said.

"So am I," said Mr. Einsbruch. "If they had been, I'd be resting a judgment on your doorstep. Anything that boy does is your fault."

"I know," I said.

"Well, that's over with. Now you can get on with things. Seen any more of that wolf of yours?"

"Have a look for yourself," I said, pointing to the tracks that remained from the night before.

"Just look at those, Pa!" Nels said. "They're the biggest tracks I've ever seen. They're bigger than that cougar we shot last year up Buffalo Draw."

"Looks more like bear tracks," Mr. Einsbruch said. "No wonder that Indian lit out. He saw his death in those tracks."

I wanted to deny it, but it certainly looked as if that was exactly what Yellow Feather had done.

I was visited by several other neighbors that next week. All of them came to see the huge tracks. Strangely enough, the wolf itself didn't return. I kept watch for it alone on the hill, but it didn't come. It was as if Yellow Feather's departure had spelled an end of the wolf, too.

Somewhere in the back of my mind, though, I knew the wolf would return. But I didn't think Yellow Feather would.

9

December struck hard at our little farm on the Brazos. I never knew winds could bring that kind of a chill to a man's bones. Then came the ice, long, freezing sheets of it.

Travis and I worked ourselves half to death getting the remains of our cattle herded into the barn during an ice storm. In August we'd had twenty-five cows, a big bull, and a few calves. Now we only had eighteen head all put together. Pa would be disappointed I'd not been able to keep more of them alive.

Travis was eleven years old now, but he still was only a whisper of a boy. The cold cut right through him, and though he never said anything, I could see the tears in his eyes as the wind bit into him. Once we got the cattle into the barn, I sat down beside him.

"Life's hard, huh, Travis?" I asked him.

"Yeah," he sighed. "Awful hard sometimes."

"Let's get you out of that shirt," I said.

"I'll freeze," Travis objected.

"No, it'll be all right," I told him, helping him out of his soggy coat and frozen cotton shirt.

"You never complain," I said to him. "You must be half frozen to death."

"It's just as hard on you," Travis said. "You never complain either. You have to take care of all of us, and you never say anything."

"I'm almost a man," I said. "You're a boy still. You shouldn't have to work so hard. If you push yourself like this, we'll be digging you a grave before spring."

"You think so?" Travis asked, his eyes full of sorrow. "Sometimes I feel so tired I want to fall asleep right where I am. I know if I did that, I'd die of cold. But it just doesn't seem to matter."

"I've felt that way, Travis. But you have to fight on. You have to battle all the way."

"I heard Grandma Clinton say one time she felt the hand of death on her. I think I must have, too. It was icy cold, like the wind out there. It cut right through the heart of me. But I fought it off."

"You're a good man to have around," I said, taking a spare shirt I had in the barn and rubbing his back vigorously. "You'll never know how much you've helped. But it can't go on like this, Travis. You're going to have to take it easier."

"How can I?" Travis asked.

"The cattle are all in the barn now. From now on your job will be to feed and water them. Old Cactus, too. That'll keep you out of the wind."

"That means you'll have to chop all the firewood, check the fences, and take care of the hogs. That's too much," Travis complained.

"No." I smiled at him, pulling him toward me. "Little brother, you'll do your share. When you get a little stronger, you'll do more. Now let me get you into this dry shirt."

I slipped the shirt over his thin shoulders and watched the shine come back to his eyes. When I pulled my big coat over him his surprised eyes lit up.

"That's your coat," he said.

"You need it right now," I said. "You ready to run to the house?"

"Yeah," he smiled. "But you'll freeze without a coat."

"It'll only be a little while. When you're inside, I'll get the coat and finish the chores."

Travis leaned against me. "Thanks, T.J.," he said in a soft voice.

"That's okay."

As we walked to the door of the barn, Travis stumbled. I helped him up, seeing just how tired he really was. We'd been at it since dawn, and here it was now, nearly dusk. He'd eaten nothing all that time. I picked him up in my arms and felt how limp he was. Then I started across the farmyard to the house.

The wind slashed us, ripping the shirt from my back. I felt the cold bite into me, but I gritted my teeth and fought back the pain. I held Travis close to me, feeling his feeble arms clutch my shoulders. I felt anger for all the harshness winter had brought as I battled my way across the yard.

Finally, the door of the house opened, and I stumbled inside, Travis held firmly in my arms.

"Thank God you're all right, boys," Ma said. "I've never in all my born days seen a storm the likes of this one."

"Is there any hot water for a bath for Travis?" I said. "He's awful cold, and I'm afraid he's going to come down with a fever."

"T.J.," Travis said faintly. "Thanks. I'll be all right."

"You'd better be, Travis. You know I need you around the place."

"Sure, T.J."

I got him into the bed he shared with Austin. His clothes were damp, but my coat had kept most of the ice off him. His boots and socks were soaked, though.

"I'm sorry to be so much trouble, T.J.," Travis said.

"You're no trouble, Travis. Pa used to do this for me when I was little. You hang in there, and we'll get you warm."

Ma brought in a pail of hot water, and I bathed Travis's cold little body. His skin was so pale it brought tears to my eyes. I wanted to curse the weather, curse the war, curse the whole world. But I found myself too busy with Travis to do any of that.

"Feel better?" I asked him, starting to soap his back.

"Yeah," he sighed. "I'm not so cold anymore."

"Can you feel your fingers and your toes?" I asked.

"Kinda. They feel funny, though."

I finished bathing him, then started rubbing his arms and legs. Pa told me once that you could work the life back into someone who was really cold by rubbing their limbs. It seemed to work on Travis because as I rubbed, color returned to his arms and legs. When I'd finished, I dressed him in his warmest clothes, put him in his bed, covered him with a couple of blankets, and sat down beside the bed.

"How do you feel now?" I asked him.

"Like a king," he said. "I'm not so cold anymore."

"You're a brave little soldier," I said, patting him on the shoulder. "You mind your manners, and Ma'll have you up and around again in no time."

"Am I sick?" Travis asked me.

"No," I said. "Just tired, I think."

"I'm going to be sick, though, aren't I?"

"I expect so. You can't go get yourself half frozen without being a little sick. You'll be all right, though. Captain's orders."

"Are you coming in now?" he asked.

"As soon as I tend to the firewood," I said.

"Be careful, T.J.," Travis said. "We need you."

I smiled at him as I closed the door to his room. I thought to myself that in a way Travis was as much a man as most men ever get to be.

The days got longer and longer for me after that. Travis did get sick, running a fever that got so high it worried me. Ma and I washed him down three times a day, but he ate nothing except soup. He just sort of shriveled up like a dried grape.

The girls took care of the cows and the hogs. I got the firewood supply caught up and mended the fences that had blown down. We lost another cow—it had to be killed after an accident—so we had fresh meat for a while. But as the winter wore on, I felt myself slipping.

I never got warm anymore. My brothers and sisters all slept in the big front room, where we kept the fire burning. Ma and I kept to our rooms, but they were cold, and sleep was hard to come by.

The week before Christmas Travis finally got well enough to walk around some. I had spent all my spare time making some buckskin clothes for him. Although I'd planned to give them to him on Christmas, I decided he needed a lift more right then.

Travis put them on, looking like a frontiersman for sure. They were warm, too, and they sped his recovery.

My own clothes were getting awfully ragged. I had

one pair of buckskin trousers, which were rough and warm, but I didn't have a single shirt that kept out the cold. Pa's old coat was pretty worn, too, and my boots had great holes in the soles.

Then, the day before Christmas, Nels Einsbruch rode over with a bag of presents.

"Oh, Nels, we have so little to give in return," Ma said. "Only some preserves for your ma, and a new dress I made for Bertha. You and your pa will have to do with some cotton handkerchiefs."

"Thank you kindly, Mrs. Clinton," Nels said. "I've brought some lace for the girls and yourself, a new coat for Travis, and a little wagon for Austin. It was mine, and I had great fun with it once. For you," he said, turning to me, "Pa made something special. Here are your new boots, sir," Nels said, handing me a pair of handsome black leather boots. "I also brought you a coat that was Hermann's. He doesn't need it now, and I'm sure you do."

"Thanks, Nels," I said in a choked voice. "Merry Christmas."

"Merry Christmas, everyone," Nels shouted to the family.

"Merry Christmas, Nels," the girls and Ma shouted back.

"Merry Christmas, Nels," said Travis.

"Tell your family many thanks," Ma said. "I hope we'll all be able to share a grand old Christmas with you next year."

"Yes, ma'am," Nels said. "I do, too."

As I walked outside to help him get to his horse, Nels grabbed my arm.

"There's something I have to talk to you about, T.J.," he said.

"Sure, Nels, What can I do for you?"

"That wolf of yours is back. It killed a bull of ours up in our north pasture just two nights ago. The Hills lost three goats the week before."

"I thought it would come back," I said. "We have all our cattle in the barn, though. What's left of them, I mean. The winter's been so hard we haven't got much left."

"We want to raise a posse and go after that wolf. With snow on the ground, it shouldn't be too hard to track it."

"You know I'd go if things were better," I said. "But, Nels, Travis is too weak to chop firewood, and the girls can't do that kind of work. My family has to come first."

"I know," Nels said. "Pa told me I shouldn't even ask. But you're the best at tracking animals I know of, and we'll need someone like you. I told Pa you'd tell me if you couldn't come. You just did."

"Nels," I said, turning him around. "Once the weather breaks, that wolf will be back here. Then I'll take it. I hope you kill it before then because one man doesn't have much of a chance against it. But if it comes back here, it's my intention to kill it."

"You'd be a fool to try all by yourself."

"I'd be a fool to let it eat our livestock and starve us all. I got a slug into it once. This time I'll get it for good."

"Maybe," Nels said.

Nels rode off down the road, and I feared for him and the others. I wasn't convinced that creature wasn't the devil Yellow Feather had called it, and I was more than a little afraid of it. Still, it seemed that wolf became the symbol of all the struggles I was facing to keep us alive. My hatred of it grew stronger than my fear, and I got to where I welcomed its return to our farm.

The final week of December, Nels rode back.

"T.J., the wolf's heading your way. It's been killing cattle near your north fences."

"Did you find it?" I asked.

"Joel Harmon gave it a nasty scrape across its forehead. I put three slugs into its hide, but it was like nothing happened. We couldn't even find any blood. And that beast killed three of the finest hunting dogs in the county."

"You didn't believe me when I told you I'd shot it."

"I believe a cannon couldn't kill that thing. I just hope it goes away."

"It won't," I mumbled. "It's here to test our courage," I said as Nels turned his horse.

"You don't believe that Comanche rot, do you?" he asked me.

"Maybe," I said. "I knew the last time I saw those eyes that they'd be coming for me."

"I hope you're wrong. Good luck, T.J."

"Sure, Nels," I said, hoping I was wrong, too.

10

We didn't have much time to celebrate the new year that winter. The heaviest snowfall in memory hit on the last day of December. Travis had been getting around pretty well, but I still didn't trust his frail body against the harsh winter. The girls couldn't hope to get through the deep snows, either. That meant I had to tend to all of the animals myself and bring in enough firewood for several days.

My new boots kept the cold away from my feet, but the coat the Einsbruchs had sent was never meant for such a winter. I felt the cold cut deep into my shoulders, and my lungs ached as I tried to inhale the freezing air.

When I'd finally fought my way through the snow to the barn, I grabbed the pitchfork and forked fresh hay for the cattle. As I worked, Cactus came over and nuzzled my face.

"Old Cactus," I said to the horse. "You're old and tired, but today you'd give a bale of hay for a good crisp run through the snow, wouldn't you?"

Cactus whinnied, dropping his head as if he knew what I'd said.

I walked around the barn, noticing that the cattle seemed to be doing better. The girls had done a good job of feeding them. Even the two little calves were growing stronger.

"I think we'll lick you, winter," I cried out. "You may have given us a tough going over, but we're stronger than you thought. Even snow and ice won't keep us down."

As I spoke, a blast of wind shook the barn, and the snow started falling all over again. I thought to myself that the winter was reminding me we hadn't survived just yet.

With the cattle fed, I shoveled some snow into the water trough. The snow would melt, and the cattle would be able to drink. Finished, I opened the barn door and challenged the cold.

Closing the barn door, I felt the icy wind sting my face. I struggled through the snowdrifts, my feet kicking up the white powder. As I reached the wood-pile, my fingers grew numb. I swept the snow away from the top of the pile. Then I took the logs in my arms, my fingers aching terribly.

When I got a full load of logs into my arms, I plowed my way to the front door. Travis pulled the door open, and I stacked the logs in the doorway.

"Aren't you coming in?" Travis asked.

"After I bring in two more loads," I told him.

"You'll freeze," said Hope. "It's too cold."

"If I don't do it now, I won't later, either," I said, walking back to the woodpile.

Two more times I struggled my way to the door with an armful of logs. I felt my fingers throb with the cold. When I returned for the third time I stumbled inside, dropping the logs with a bang on the floor.

"You should have come in earlier," Ma scolded me.

"I couldn't," I said. "It had to be done."

"You're worse than me," Travis told me. "Come on back to your room. Ma, get some hot water."

I laughed at him.

"I'm not that bad off yet," I smiled. "But you're all right, little brother."

"I'm just doing what you did for me," he told me.

"I know," I said. "It's nice to know you're around in case I need it."

As I stood up, Hope and Travis picked up the logs and carried them to the fireplace. I stripped tbe gloves from my swollen fingers, wincing with pain.

"Let me rub your hands," said Ma, shaking her head. "You're lucky if you don't get frostbite."

"Thanks. Pa always used to rub them for me to keep away the frostbite," I said. "It always works."

"Sure. Only next time don't take such risks."

It was an unnecessary warning. The weather lifted, and the rest of January was better. But with the improved weather came new problems.

The biggest problem was that half our fences had been blown down by the fierce winds. I rode out daily on old Cactus, nailing barbed wire back into place and replacing broken posts. Toward the end of the month, Travis felt well enough to go with me, and with him along again, I realized how much I had missed his company.

We talked about a hundred things, but mainly about life. Many of the things Travis said surprised me. Once he told me how much easier it is to sacrifice your own wishes when it will help someone you love to get his. I knew he was talking about me, and it was nice to know he realized what I was doing. More important, I knew he was prepared to do the same thing if something happened to me.

Then, the last night of January, everything changed. I was sleeping pleasantly when I heard a loud banging in the barn.

"What's happening?" I yelled.

"There's something in the barn," screamed Rachel. "I think it's after Cactus."

I grabbed my pants and pulled them on. Slipping my arms into my coat, I raced to the gun cabinet.

"You want me to come, too?" asked a sleepy Travis.

"Stay in the house, Travis," I told him. "But be ready to shoot."

"I will," he said, picking out a rifle.

I made my way to the barn, listening to the sounds of the cattle's bodies banging against the walls of their stalls. Over it all came the angry snorts of Cactus.

I saw now that the door of the barn was slightly open. I pushed it open all the way and peered inside. It was too dark to see anything, but I entered and walked slowly along the outside wall, cautiously pointing the gun away from me.

As my eyes grew accustomed to the dark, I saw Cactus. The old horse shook, his mouth full of froth. But he was all right. Then I saw what I had already feared. A pair of fiery red eyes looked in my direction.

"Devil beast," I said under my breath. "I knew you would come. One of us is bound to die, and I don't intend for it to be me."

The wolf growled, flashing his teeth in the moonlight. I trembled, feeling a chill that was not in the air. Then I carefully slid the cartridge into the gun and waited for my chance. Before I could fire, though, the wolf darted out the door and melted into the darkness.

I lit a lantern and inspected the damage. Miraculously, only Cactus was hurt. The old horse had fought the wolf, but there were only a few scratches on the horse's legs. I tended to them before going back to bed.

The next night the wolf returned. I rushed to get dressed, but I was too late. All I saw of the beast were those two fierce eyes peering at me from the night. Then it raced off with two chickens.

The next morning, I stood up at the breakfast table.

"The wolf will not simply go away," I said. "I'm going to chop enough firewood to get you into spring. Then I'm going after that beast."

"I'll go, too," said Travis.

"No," I said. "It's not that I don't want you, Travis. You know how much I'd like to have you along. But you've got to stay home. Ma needs you here."

"What do I have to do?" Travis asked.

"Without me home, practically everything. You'll have to tend the animals and bring water up to the house. If the wolf comes, you'll have to protect the house. I wouldn't leave if I didn't think things were in good hands. I know you'll do your best."

"I will," murmured Travis.

"You girls," I said, turning to Abigail, Rachel, and Hope, "will have to do the rest. Travis is only eleven, and there are so many things he can't do by himself.

You'll have to help him, especially with the animals. The hogs, chickens, and cattle must be fed and watered. You can do that."

"We will, T.J.," the girls said.

"And I'll take care of the wolf," I announced.

As I packed a knapsack with food, Ma pulled me off to one corner.

"You really have to go, don't you?" she asked.

"You know I do," I said.

"Take great care, Thomas," she added. "I didn't raise you fourteen years to have you die in a deer thicket or river bottom."

"Ma," I said. "I don't want to die. But if I have to, then I'm ready. Sure, I would like to grow up, live to a ripe old age. But you know that to have things, you have to fight for them. That's why Pa went to Tennessee to fight for General Hood. I have to do what I have to do, same as him."

"Son," Ma said, crying. "We never been really close. You keep to yourself so much. You're not outgoing like Jackson and Houston. Or even Travis. And yet you're everything I could have wished for in a son—strong, brave, willing to do for others."

"It's what you and Pa have always taught me."

"You've made us proud, Thomas. Fight this wolf and return to us. We need you."

As I turned away, I remembered Travis saying almost those same words. They were about the best words I could remember anyone had said about me.

I went next to the small room Travis and Austin shared. I kissed little Austin on the cheek and accepted his hug. Then I shook hands with Travis, my big little brother. Quickly Travis threw his arms around me and gave me a hug, too.

"Don't grow up too fast," I told him. "I'm coming back."

"Be careful, T.J.," he said. "I love you."

"I love you, too," I said, shaking away a tear. "Good-bye."

The girls were harder to say good-bye to. Travis understood what I was doing and why. Austin was too little to care. The girls knew I was taking a chance, but they didn't want me to go. I loved them all very much, and I found myself surrounded by their arms.

There were tears in all our eyes when I told them I had to leave. They hung on to me, begging me to stay.

"I'm coming back, so don't cry for me yet," I told them.

"Are you really coming back?" asked Abigail, who had just turned twelve. "Pa and Houston and Jackson haven't come back yet. I don't want any of you to die."

"They'll be back, too," I said. "And I'll be here to greet them."

My last good-bye was saved for Grandma Nelson. She simply kissed me and said nothing. She'd faced the uncertainty of winter many times, and her quiet confidence gave me strength.

Swallowing deeply, I stepped forward and closed the door behind me. I had my knapsack over one shoulder and my rifle over the other. I kept my eyes fixed on the wolf's tracks, shedding any feeling of fear as I sang an old song Pa had taught me.

The road ahead might be full of danger, but I faced it with confidence, knowing I could handle anything that came in my way.

11

I hoped to locate the wolf's lair by daylight. But his tracks were everywhere, and I was misled several times before I finally found the true trail. By that time, the sun was already dying in the west, and the wind whistled through the juniper trees in a ghostly manner.

I held my rifle ever ready, prepared for a sudden charge by the devil beast. But the more I walked, the quieter the woods became. It was almost as if there was no wolf. But something within me told me it was out there, waiting for me even as I had waited for it on the hill overlooking the farm.

As I walked, darkness closed in all around me. I took the bits of dried beef from my knapsack and chewed them. I hadn't realized how hungry a person could get. I was glad I could eat because it took my mind off the wolf.

But the beef was soon gone, and my eyes searched the darkness for the terrible red eyes I knew were there. Every time a bird stirred or the wind rustled through the leaves, my heart pounded, and I swung the rifle in that direction.

Finally, halfway up a hill, I came to a great mound of rocks that blazed white in the early moonlight. It was a chilling place, and as I stared at it, a low growl came from the rocks. I raised my rifle just as the great beast, its silvery coat brilliant in the moonlight, climbed upon the tallest of the rocks and glared down at me.

"Our time has come," I called to the wolf. "One of us will not leave this place."

As if it understood, the wolf let out a great, mournful howl.

"You should sing a death chant in the way of the Comanche," I shouted. "For your death is in my hands this very instant."

As I spoke, the wolf bounded from the rocks and charged me. I braced myself against a tree and swung the rifle around so that its sight held the wolf squarely. I remembered what Pa had taught me about firing at an animal.

"Wait for the leap," he had said. "Once an animal is in the air, it cannot change directions. You fire too early, your shot is missed and you're helpless."

I waited for the right moment. The wolf moved like lightning, and it was upon me before I knew it. As it leaped, it filled the air with its snarling sound. I paused one second, then fired.

The air exploded with the blast of the rifle, but I had no time to listen. I was hit by the full force of the charging wolf, and I fell to the ground, clutching blindly at my rifle.

Those vicious red eyes were right in front of me, and suddenly I felt the wolf sink its teeth into my left arm. Pain shot through every inch of me, and I felt blood pour out of a gash in my side. I saw the wolf, too, was bleeding, but it didn't matter. In another minute, I would be dead.

Then the air filled with another sound. It was like the call of a screech owl, and whatever made it moved like a hawk diving at its prey. The wolf pulled away, torn from my broken body by I didn't know what. I managed to sit up, my left arm limp with pain. With my good right arm I reached for the rifle.

As my eyes cleared, I saw before me a terrible sight. The wolf had pinned something beneath it. Whatever, or whoever, had come to my rescue could not live long if I didn't bring the wolf back to me.

I slid a cartridge into the rifle and closed the bolt.

Then I shook my head clear of the pain and brought the sights to bear. Finally, I squeezed the trigger, blowing a hole in the side of the wolf.

The creature turned, its eyes blood-red with anger. As it moved toward me, I saw what had taken its attention. Getting to his feet was Yellow Feather, my friend, my companion. And I thought he'd deserted me.

I remembered for a second what he'd said about the legend. Only two warriors of pure heart and courage could kill that wolf. Well, here we were, ready to take the life of the beast.

I tried to reload the rifle, but my eyes grew foggy, and the shell slipped through my fingers. The wolf hit hard, and I tumbled down the hill. The right side of my face was warm with blood, and one of my eyes was closed. I could feel blood running into my mouth, and I felt my shirt being ripped away.

I reached my right hand back to my belt, grabbing my hunting knife. As the wolf sank its teeth into my side, I stabbed with all the fury I could manage.

The wolf howled in pain as I stabbed its neck. I felt the blood flow over my hand as I stabbed a second time. Then the wolf was struck by something else, and it left me, twisting and bleeding, but hanging on to life. I saw a Comanche lance hanging from the side of the creature.

Yellow Feather limped down the hill. He was singing a chant. I'd heard it before, sung by the old warrior at the battle last fall. It was the Comanche death chant, and something gnawed at my heart. I struggled to get to my feet, but there was not enough strength in me, and I fell back down. I felt my rifle, but the stock was smashed, and my eyes were too clouded to load it anyway.

Yellow Feather waited for the wolf, holding a knife out in front of him. The wolf, its side torn open by the lance, its neck carved by my knife, two bullets in its chest, leaped forward.

For what seemed an eternity, the wolf hung in the air. Then Yellow Feather swung his knife into its belly, and the two of them rolled into a single ball of fur and boy.

I listened to the sound of the wolf snarling and slashing the naked flesh of my friend. I stumbled forward, the life force of me flowing down into my legs. At last, I saw the Indian raise his arm and plunge the knife down in one final motion. The wolf stirred no more.

I crawled over to Yellow Feather. His eyes burned with the fire I'd known before. But his face was pale with death, and I saw his chest and belly were ripped open by the wolf. There was nothing I could do, but I took his hand and tried somehow to give him some of the life that still fought on within me.

"Amigos," Yellow Feather whispered.

"Yes," I said. "Friends. We killed the beast, the Diablo Argentino."

99

"Diablo killed," Yellow Feather sighed. "Great thing we do."

"You did it," I said, tears coming to my eyes.

"You do, too, Tee Jaaay," he whispered.

"I'll get you back to the farm," I told him. "We can patch you up. Hold on to your life."

But my words were useless. His chest was still. I fought with my right hand to wipe the blood and tears from my eyes. They were clouded and on fire. When I was finally able to see, I saw the silence that was written on his face.

"If there are such things as spirits of the Comanches," I called out, "take the spirit of Yellow Feather, my friend. He was brave and true of heart. He should have lived long. I should be the one who lies here dead, and I would be, were it not for him."

I paused a moment.

"He was the bravest, the strongest," I sobbed. "He was my friend."

I tried to stand up, but there was no feeling left in my legs. There was a big wound in my side, blood flowing over my waist and legs. I slid over and touched Yellow Feather's hand. It was not yet cold.

"Good-bye, my friend," I said.

Then the pain shot up my spine from the gashes in my side and thigh, and I knew only a world of darkness.

12

I never knew exactly how long I lay wounded beside the body of my friend, Yellow Feather, and the remains of the great silver wolf. When I didn't return by morning, Travis had saddled Cactus and ridden to the Einsbruch farm to get help.

They'd searched for hours. Nels finally found me, bloody and unconscious, and they'd first thought I was dead. But little Travis had taken my hand and announced there was life within me yet.

I'd lost a lot of blood, and my head didn't clear for days. I remember finally seeing something fuzzy above me, and I moved my right hand out, grasping for my rifle.

"It's all right," I heard the sweet voice of my sister Hope say. "You're safe, T.J. You're in your bed at home."

I shook my head to bring my eyes into focus, but I still couldn't see well.

"Ma says you're not supposed to move your head," Hope told me. "You may have a concussion, and the ride back here in Mr. Einsbruch's wagon didn't help."

"Mr. Einsbruch's wagon?" I moaned. "When? Why?"

"Travis got them to help look for you," Hope explained. "He's really taken charge around here. I believe any day he's going to start growing a beard and take your place as head of the household."

"Where's Yellow Feather?" I asked. "What . . ."

"Nels Einsbruch buried him on the hill," she told me. "Travis told them it's what you'd want them to do. Mr. Einsbruch wasn't much in favor of the idea, but it was pretty clear to everyone that the two of you had fought that wolf together. We all thought Yellow Feather had gone, you know."

"So did I," I said. "I would have been dead if he hadn't charged that wolf. You should have seen him. He just stood there with a knife in his hand, waiting for the wolf to charge. He was singing the Comanche death chant. He knew he was going to die. He did it to save my life."

"Why?" she asked. "That's crazy."

"It was his way," I said. "We were friends. When he told me about the wolf, he told me it could only be killed by two young warriors of pure heart and great courage. And he said something else that he never explained. He said it would take a great sacrifice. He made the great sacrifice. He gave his life."

"How sad," Hope said. "He was always nice to us, even though we were scared silly by him. Travis really liked him."

"Yes," I sighed. "Where is Travis?"

"Out with the cows," Hope said. "He and Rachel tend them while Ma and I and Abigail take care of the hogs and chickens. You should see Rachel let that old bull have it when he doesn't do what he's supposed to."

"If Rachel isn't careful, that old bull will give her a good boot into the next county," I said.

"He chased her into the river yesterday. But she gave him a beating he'll not soon forget."

"Thomas, is that you talking?" Ma's voice called to me from the front room. "Is that you?"

"Yes, Ma," I said. "It's me."

"Saints be praised," Ma cried out, running into the room. "Thank God you're all right."

"I don't know how all right I am," I said, feeling sore all over. "I feel like I've been run over by a herd of cattle."

"You ought to see how you look." Hope laughed.

"How do I look?" I said seriously. "And just what's wrong with me?"

"Well, let's see," Ma said. "First of all, you've got a big gash in your left thigh I had to sew up. There's a big hole in your side we patched. Your left arm is broken, and it's got a couple of real nice slices out of it, too."

"What about my eye?" I asked. "Is it still there?"

"Your eye is fine," she said. "You've got a big cut across your forehead, though. And probably a concussion."

"Anything else?" I asked, picturing myself as a walking bandage.

"Probably some broken ribs," Hope said. "They'll be nice and sore for a while."

"My legs?" I asked.

"They're fine, but you can't walk for another week or so because of that gash in your thigh. When that heals, you should be fine."

"Sure," I grumbled. "That'll heal in another month or so."

"You're young, you'll mend fast," Ma said. "But the weather is turning, and Travis should be able to keep things going until then."

"Don't let him do too much," I said. "I don't want him working himself to death."

"Look who's talking," Ma said. "You're the one flat on his back."

"And I don't want anyone else here beside me."

104

"T.J.?" asked a high-pitched voice from the front room.

"That's me, T.J."

"Boy, am I ever glad you're all right," said Travis, running into the room and jumping on the bed.

I moaned as my ribs were jolted.

"I'm not too upset about it myself," I told him.

"You sure had us scared. When Nels found you, he yelled out that you were dead. But I knew it couldn't be. You just couldn't be dead."

Travis reached his hand over and felt my head.

"The fever's better today, too. You were on fire when we found you. There was blood all over you, and that wolf wasn't three feet from Yellow Feather. I thought for a minute he might be alive, too, but his insides were all over the place. It must have been a terrible way to die."

"He was your friend, too, Travis," I said. "He didn't die in a terrible way. He sang his death chant as the wolf charged. Then he split the beast open with his knife, killing it. He was real peaceful at the end. He called me his friend just before he died."

"And we thought he'd run away, while all that time he must have been up in the woods watching out for the wolf," Travis said.

"Yes," I agreed. "But he was really waiting for me. I guess he knew sooner or later I'd have to come after the wolf. It was part of the legend that the two of us had to fight it together."

"Yes." Travis frowned. "The two of you had to fight it, and one of you had to die."

"Did he tell you that?" I asked.

"Yes," Travis said. "He made me swear never to tell you, though. He said you'd understand when it happened."

"Yes," I sighed.

"I cut the head off and sent it in to the Rangers for the bounty. Mr. Einsbruch said Pa once got a fifty-dollar reward for killing a wolf. Fifty dollars would sure come in handy about now."

"What about the hide?" I asked.

"That's the strange part," Travis said, his eyes widening. "I cut off the paws 'cause I figured you'd want them. But I planned to go back and skin it. When I went back, there wasn't a sign of it. Just the grave where Nels buried Yellow Feather. There wasn't even any blood left from that wolf. Do you think . . ."

"That it really was a devil? That the legend was true? As strange as that animal was, it was only a wolf. Probably some other animal, a coyote maybe, hauled it away."

"That wolf was almost as big as a cow," Travis said. "I never saw a coyote or anything alive that could have hauled it off."

"Well, I sure don't believe it just vanished," I said.

"Lots of weird things have been happening. Yellow Feather comes to save your life. This big wolf we never saw before comes down to kill cattle and chickens. I don't know. It all sure seems strange."

"I can't argue with that, Travis," I said. "But I think it's just what happened that makes everybody start making up all kinds of stories. One thing I know for sure. It was Yellow Feather and me together that killed that wolf. No one man with a rifle could ever have taken it."

In the days that followed, we talked often about the wolf. Nels came by one day to visit, telling me he thought someone might have gone up there and taken the wolf for its hide.

"A wolf hide that color and size would be really something," he told me. "Never in all my life did I see a wolf with a silver coat like that one."

"I know," I said. "And I'll never forget those red eyes. They seemed to look right through you."

I grew stronger as the days flew by. By the end of the first week, Hope and Abigail had taken to helping me get up to sit in Grandma Nelson's old rocker out by the porch. There I could catch some sun. My color improved, and my wounds healed.

I was still a sorry sight, though. There were two jagged wounds on my forearm and a terrible tear in my side. My thigh had a cut halfway across and all the way down to my knee. And over my left eye was another cut about seven inches long.

"You look like you ran into a mesquite branch," Ma said, laughing.

"Am I too awful ugly?" I asked.

"No, Thomas," she said. "Just battered a bit. You're young. You'll heal."

"I'll never get a girl to look at me, though, will I?"

"Girls around here don't take to a man 'cause he's pretty in the face," Ma said. "They take to a man for what's inside. That's what those scars will mean to a girl. She'll know you're a man with something inside."

"I hope so," I said.

In another week, the injuries weren't half as bad, and my leg had healed enough for me to limp around. I was eating well, and the ribs didn't ache every time I laughed. Life was beginning to look a lot better.

13

In three weeks' time, I'd healed rather nicely. The scars would be around always, but my legs were sound, and I was gaining more and more of my strength back. Travis and the girls kept things going, but they were looking forward to having me back in charge. Little Travis was getting to be a little hard on everybody's nerves.

As my legs allowed me, I walked around the farm, seeing to those things I could. There were several fences down, and Travis couldn't put them back up. But more than mending fences was on my mind. There was something that had to be done.

One morning my feet found themselves walking aimlessly to the barn. I caught sight of Travis yelling at the chickens, and I laughed to myself. Then I walked inside the barn and put my right hand on old Cactus's nose.

"You old warhorse," I said. "You're as lively as ever. How would you like to take me on a short ride?"

Cactus snorted and stomped his feet as if he knew what I'd said.

"Come on, old horse," I said. "We've got to go visit a friend."

I pulled Cactus out and had him saddled before anyone knew about it. As I led the old horse out of the barn, Travis came running over.

"What do you think you're doing?" he demanded. "You know the orders. You're supposed to take it easy until you're well."

"Thank you, general," I said. "There's something that has to be done."

"Not by you," he objected.

"Yes," I said. "By me. Only by me. Besides, Cactus needs the exercise. This poor horse isn't getting run enough to keep him in shape. We might have another Indian raid some day. You can never tell."

"T.J., you can't ride yet. You'll fall and split yourself wide open again."

"Travis," I said, putting my hand on his shoulder. "I'm proud of the way you've taken over. But it's time I got back to work. There's something I have to do.

I'll tell you about it some time when you're a little older. For now, you have to understand that I wouldn't ride anywhere I didn't have to."

"What's the problem?" asked Ma, hearing our argument.

"No problem, Ma," I said. "Travis doesn't understand that I have somewhere to go. He's just worried about me. But he's got to understand that I have to do this one thing."

"You have to go back there, don't you." she said.

"Yes."

"Why?" Ma asked, her eyes suddenly sad.

"Because I have things to say," I said. "I don't really understand why myself, but somehow I'm not at peace. I just have to go to set my mind at rest."

"I understand," Travis said. "It's something you can't do here because you didn't lose your peace here. It has to do with what I told you Yellow Feather said, doesn't it?"

"Yes," I told him. "I don't know if there are such things as spirits or not, but I feel there's something back there that I need to speak to."

"Then go, Thomas," Ma said. "But be careful."

"I will," I said, pulling myself onto Cactus. Slowly I rode away.

It had been nearly dark when I reached the wolf's lair that day, but the way there was still clear in my mind. I found myself urging Cactus into a trot as we made our way down the road. We passed the old white oak tree with its ghostly appearance. Then we left the road and started out across the broken ground that marked the edge of our farm.

The wind whistled a mournful tune through the branches of the juniper trees as I made my way up into the rocks. When I neared the spot, I slowed Cactus. Then I slid down off the horse and tied him to a mesquite tree.

"Good boy," I whispered softly. "Good boy. I'll be back before too long."

Then I walked up the hill until I reached the pile of rocks where I'd first spotted the wolf. My eyes imagined its red eyes glaring at me once again. But the sun blazed brightly against the rocks, and my eyes cleared.

I made my way to the spot where the wolf had finally been killed, to the spot where Yellow Feather had died and where I'd crawled to share his dying moment.

"Yellow Feather, amigo," I whispered. "There is so much I have to say," I added, searching for the mound of earth that marked his grave. At last I spotted it.

"Yellow Feather," I said, sitting down beside the grave. "I don't understand. Why did you give your life for me? I am your enemy by nature. It is not natural for you to have done it."

I thought about the whole question. It bothered me. Then I remembered something he'd told me. He said that the devil spirit came to test the courage of the Comanche warriors. I guessed he thought the wolf had come not for me but for him.

He'd told me about how once three warriors had set out to kill it. The first two were brave and courageous, but the third one had fear in his heart. He ran, and all three were killed. It took the courage of all the warriors to kill the beast.

But why hadn't he mentioned the fact that the beast demanded a sacrifice? Perhaps he thought I might have offered myself. I knew better. It was because I never would have allowed him to give up his own life for mine.

"Why did he have to die, though?" I asked aloud. "He was so brave and strong. And he was just a boy trying to be a man."

I didn't understand why boys had to go to war. I didn't even understand war itself. Sure, I could understand men fighting beasts to protect their farms and their families.

But I would never understand the war my father had ridden off to. I couldn't imagine a reason for men to ride off and kill each other. Life was so simple at times and so complicated at others.

For me, life was easy to understand. You got your crops seeded on time. You saw to their watering, and you harvested them when they were ripe. You tended your livestock, and you got along with your neighbors.

But things always got complicated. There was the war far away to the east that took fathers and brothers away, killed and maimed them. That wasn't simple at all. I hoped Pa would come back and explain it all to me.

But there were things that still had to be done. I reached into my pocket and pulled out two of the wolf's huge paws.

"I don't know much about burying people, especially Comanches," I said. "But I heard Indians are usually buried with trophies of war. I don't know where your knife is. I don't know where any of your things are. But I have these paws of the silver wolf, and I'll place them here on your grave. I also have something from me, your friend. Here." I placed my best hunting knife on the grave.

Then I walked away and found an old live oak stump.

"I don't know whether Comanches mark graves," I said, "but it is our custom to do so. I'm going to carve you a marker."

I set to work with my ax, cutting the stump apart. My shoulder ached from lack of use, but I bore down harder and forgot the pain. As the ax cut away at the stump, I saw how it would make a fine marker. I didn't think a cross would be proper, but I needed a marker, something to keep the memory alive of what happened there.

Last of all, I chopped through the base of the

stump until the upper part was free. Sighing, I rolled the stump to where Yellow Feather lay buried. Then I took out my carving knife and set to work.

I carved away the rough outside and cleaned away the rough spots. Then I shaped it so the front and back were flat. Finally, I started carving the words.

"On this spot," I carved, "Yellow Feather of the Comanche nation sacrificed his life for a friend."

It took me nearly two hours to carve it all. But when I finally finished, it was a marker fit for a prince.

I knelt down on one knee and took my ax. Then I pounded the marker into the ground beside his grave. A strange silence settled around me, and I bowed my head.

"Dear Lord," I said. "Hear this prayer for my friend, Yellow Feather. I don't know much about different religions and all that. I've only been in a church a couple of times in my whole life. But I know you for the world you've made, and I think you understand the things I don't.

"This boy who's buried here, Yellow Feather, I never saw him do anything evil. I don't know that he believed in you the way I do, but I know he trusted in a Great Spirit, and that must be you, too. He was a good boy, and he sacrificed himself for me and my family. I can't think of anything a man can do that's better than that. So if you have a little time, Lord, would you keep an eye out for Yellow Feather? Guide his soul to the kind of peace Pa always told me a man could find in death if his life has been the way you wanted it to be."

I stood up and looked around me. The sun was dipping into a horizon filled with clouds, and there was already a chill in the air. I wiped away a tear and said my last good-bye. Then I walked to where Cactus was grazing.

"Well, old horse," I said. "It's time to go home."

As I untied the reins and mounted Cactus, I knew I'd come back here many times. But it would never again be as a boy. For somehow I had buried my childhood back there with Yellow Feather.

Back home things went back to the way they were before I'd ever heard of Comanche Indians or silver devils. Travis and I tended the cattle and mended the fences. The girls took care of the chickens and hogs.

We had a little easier time because the Texas Rangers gave a hundred-dollar bounty on the wolf, which paid for some badly needed clothing and several new tools.

At last the winter gave way to spring, and the trees broke out their leaves. Flowers sprang to life. And there were rumors that men were returning home from the war.

14

Spring brought the usual rains to the Brazos Valley. Sheets and sheets of rain washed the dust from the roads, from the barn and house, even from the rocky countrysides. It seemed to lend everything a freshness, a newness.

I'd dreaded the coming of spring, for it was planting time. The corn crop could go in late, but the other vegetables had to be planted, as well as the feed crops for the cattle. It was too much work for Travis and me, and I'd hoped Pa and Houston and Jackson would be back in time. They weren't.

The garden was the easier part. We took the small

plow out of the barn and rigged the harness around my shoulders. A small mule would have worked better, but we had none. Travis guided the plow as I struggled to move the blade through the rocky soil.

Every year we moved rock after rock from the garden, but the next year there were always more. I never understood why the earth was so hard on farmers.

Though I had sharpened the plow blade, I strained to move it each foot. Sweat poured out of my skin, running down my back so that it seemed as though I'd been swimming. Each morning I broke enough soil for the girls to seed. Each evening, I turned a little more.

It was work for a grown man. But it had to be done by me, and I gritted my teeth and did it. Sometimes Travis and I would sing songs to lift our spirits. The songs took our minds off the work.

Then, when the sun blazed down on us, we'd shed our clothes and dive into the river. Travis was half fish anyway, and it was a chance for me to feel young and free again for a change.

By the beginning of May, we'd planted the whole garden. It could now be tended by Ma and the girls. The feed crop was in, too. Only the corn crop awaited us, but it was twice the challenge.

I hitched old Cactus to the big plow, wondering if the old beast would last. We had plowed thirty furrows the year before, and Travis and I meant to try for that again. The first week went well, and we got the first ten rows seeded. But then the rains returned, and the work was delayed and delayed.

Time was against us, and I began to doubt Pa would ever return. Travis tired too easily in the heat, and I often worked alone for up to fifteen hours. I would work until I dropped. Twice I slept in the fields.

When we got the twentieth row planted, things took a turn for the worse. Old Cactus, who had survived the hard winter, the attack by the wolf, and half a dozen other dangers, broke a leg. It took the heart out of me to have to shoot that old horse, but there was nothing else to do.

When we had completed the planting, we all breathed easier. Men were returning every day from the east, telling of the great defeat the Southern armies had suffered at the hands of the Yankees.

We asked everyone for information about Pa and the boys, but no one had any. Pa had fought in Tennessee, and the boys coming home had all fought somewhere else.

One night toward the end of May, I went outside all alone and looked up at the stars.

"God," I said. "I know you're up there looking down on us. Please bring Pa and my brothers home. We need them."

It couldn't have been more than a week later that Jim Hudson rode up to our farm with news.

"Boy, I fought beside your pa at Franklin," he said. "Your pa and the boys was all fine then. I expect them to come riding on home any day now."

"Hurray!" I shouted, almost afraid to imagine what it would be like to have them home again.

"Now, boy," Jim said. "They might be shot up a bit. The Texas regiments took a pretty big piece of the action around Atlanta. But I just know your pa got through it. He was one of the few who knew how to soldier. They made him a captain at Franklin."

"Did you see him?" I asked. "When was that?"

"Back in November."

"That's a long time."

"Long time on the battle line. But good men are hard to kill," he told me.

"Sure."

As he rode off, I thought of all the good men I knew who'd been killed that year. Yellow Feather had been a good man. It wasn't all that hard to kill him. Hermann Einsbruch had been a good man. He'd died awfully easy. No, good men were usually the very first to die.

Just when I'd almost given up on Pa, though, one day I came back from mending some fences to see a beautiful black horse tied up in front of our barn. I knew it was someone special, for I'd never seen such a fine horse before.

My feet took to the wind, and I raced into the

house. My eyes searched the room until they found a tall man in a tattered gray uniform. He had the torn braid of an officer on his sleeves, but there was a familiar look about him.

"Pa?" I asked, waiting for the man to turn toward me.

"T.J.?" he asked, facing me at last.

He had a full beard, and his eyes were tired. But I saw beneath it all that he was my father, and I ran to him.

"Pa," I said, burying my head in his chest.

"You didn't miss me, did you, boy?" he asked.

"Every day," I said, drying a tear that had made its way across my cheek. "Every single day and every single night."

"T.J.," Pa said. "I'm the one who went to war, but you're the one who's got the scars. Whatever happened to you, boy?"

"We had a wolf here, Pa," I said. "I had a friend who was a Comanche Indian. Together we killed the wolf, but my friend died. I was pretty torn up myself."

"Slow down, T.J." Pa laughed. "This sounds like a tall tale to me. Let's sit down a minute and you can tell me all about it."

"Well, sir," I began. "It all began with a big raid the Comanches were making on all the settlements."

"Heard about that up at Fort Worth," he said.

"Quite a few good men and women killed out near there. More than a few boys and girls, too."

"We ambushed the ones that came here. Only one of them survived, a boy about my age named Yellow Feather."

"He brought that boy home with him," Hope said.

"Who's telling this story?" I asked, standing up. "It's me that got clawed. It's my right to tell it."

"Go on, son," Pa said. "No one's gonna stop you."

"Yellow Feather was nearly dead. I nursed him back to health. He did a lot of things around the farm. He was a big help. Then this silver wolf came down and started raiding the farm. We were out waiting on it one night, and Yellow Feather disappeared."

"You're lucky he didn't disappear with your scalp," Pa said. "Go on."

"About a month later, the wolf raided us again. I took out after it. When I finally found it, it nearly killed me. Then Yellow Feather came out of nowhere. He gave his life so that I could live."

"You should have seen that wolf," said Travis. "We got a hundred-dollar bounty from the Rangers for it!"

"Never heard of a hundred-dollar bounty on a wolf before," Pa said. "Must have been a sizable wolf."

"The bounty sure helped us get through the winter," I said. "It bought seed and harness, not to mention clothes. I can tell you we were getting a little threadbare around here."

"You've done some growing, T.J.," Pa said. "I can't tell you how proud I am of you," he added, hugging me. "I knew I could trust you to see to things."

"Travis and the girls helped, too," I said.

All this time I'd been looking for Houston and Jackson. Neither one of them was to be seen. I didn't really want to hear an answer, but I felt bound to ask about them.

"Are Houston and Jackson coming tomorrow?" I asked at last.

"No, T.J.," Pa said.

"What happened to them? Are they . . . ?" My voice failed me, and I put my head into my hands. "Good people are always the first to go."

"I don't know what you're talking about," Pa said, "but your brothers were both healthy as hogs when I left them last week. Houston got married to a little French gal in New Orleans, and Jackson stayed there to go into business with him. I wanted them to come back here first, but they told me the farm wasn't big enough for five boys, and they might not have such a good opportunity next year. This way you and Travis and Austin can split the land when the time comes."

"Things could be a lot worse," I said.

"Sure they could," Pa said. "But we're all back together safe and sound. And the scars of war have a way of healing themselves. You can be more of a boy for a while, and Travis can go back to being lazy."

"Ah, Pa," Travis said. "Just 'cause I like to fish."

"And swim and run off every time there's work to be done," said Hope. "Like right now. It's time to slop the hogs."

We all laughed as Travis tried to worm his way out of the work. In the end, though, he went right out and did it.

As I settled into bed that night, I thought back on all the things that had happened to me that year. I would never be as carefree again as I'd been this time last year, but that was the way of life.

I'd learned so many things. I'd learned to accept danger and face up to a great enemy. I'd learned to trust in other people. I'd learned what it means to lose a friend. I'd seen the very real face of death. But I'd come through it all, and now I felt that there was really little left for me to fear in life.

I walked my world with straight shoulders and proud eyes, for I hadn't backed down to the challenges life had thrown my way. I'd proved to everyone who mattered that I was a man.